TALIA SUROVA

CALL ME SAFFRON

<u>Other Works by Talia Surova:</u>
Draw Me In (Greenpoint Artists prequel novella)
Hold Me Tight (Greenpoint Artists Book One)
What's Yours is Mine

www.TaliaSurova.com
talia@taliasurova.com

This is a work of fiction. Names, characters, businesses, places, events and incidents are either the products of the author's imagination or used in a fictitious manner. Any resemblance to actual persons, living or dead, or actual events is purely coincidental.

To Dan

Chapter One

I'd been picking up on the signals for a while, but I thought I'd sent enough *not interested, thanks* signals back to get the point across and forestall the Big Approach.

Apparently not. Rudy came over to my workstation as I slid the large blueprint into its protective portfolio and turned to my computer, preparing to put work onto a flash drive to take home.

He started picking up random items from my drafting table: a soft eraser, a drafting pencil, a ruler. It was like he'd already forgotten why he'd wandered over.

I tried to help him out. "Did you have more thoughts about the Rockland mall project? I thought Fernando covered the specs pretty thoroughly, but—"

Rudy put the ruler down and blurted, "Would you go out with me?"

I blinked at him. Dumbfounded, though logically I shouldn't have been.

His mouth curved into a winning smile as he recovered his poise. "So? What do you think? Dinner in the East Village, a movie after? I know you don't have plans tonight." He gestured toward my leather bag, the flash drive in my hand.

Rudy was a handsome man. Smart too. He wore

great sweaters and had the best shoes. His hair had blond streaks from summer sports and winters spent skiing. And he'd been known to quote Yeats at staff meetings. He'd be easy to hang out with.

Panic rose in my chest, making it hard to breathe. "No. I can't."

He looked disconcerted. "How about next week? I can get last-minute tickets to *Book of Mormon*. Great seats too. I have a friend on the show."

To avoid his gaze, I fit the flash drive into the port and started copying files. "No. Stop asking. Please. I'm not going to date you."

His forehead wrinkled; his mouth twisted. "Wow, I knew you had a rep for bluntness, but come on. I thought we liked each other."

Damn. I had to give him more. "We do. I do. You're a good guy. Cute, even."

His forehead uncreased. "Then why?"

"I don't date. I just don't."

"Not ever?"

"Never." You couldn't shut men off with a flick of a switch after your orgasm. And when they told you they loved you, God help you if you didn't say you loved them back.

"So you're saying it's not me, it's you?"

"I'm not relationship material." I put up my hand to forestall the retort I could see coming. "And I don't do one-night stands. It's too messy. Doubly so since we work together."

"Your loss, babe." He winked at me. At least his pride was intact.

"Don't I know it."

Download finished, I ejected the flash drive. Time to go home.

And if I sat on the A train with my legs crossed, thinking about the sex I wasn't having, my favorite vibrator waited in my nightstand drawer. It wasn't a man's warm body against mine, but it would suffice.

Things got strange when I arrived home. The living room was dead quiet, for one thing. No roommate dancing around in her underwear or doing calisthenics while cursing at the perky on-screen instructor.

I set my briefcase down. "Jeanine! Are you home?"

"In my room!"

I went into her bedroom to find her bundled under the comforter, an empty soup bowl on her nightstand, and, oddly, her work gear spread out on the bottom of the bed: a cock ring, fur-lined handcuffs, a blindfold…

"I'm sick." She sounded pathetic, her voice a weak thread.

"And you thought a little sex action would help you feel better? Sorry, I don't swing that way."

"I have a new client tonight." It was nearly a wail.

"I hate to break it to you, but you're going to have to cancel." Jeanine was a high-priced call girl. At first, she worked through an escort service, but these days she got clients by referral only. She claimed the job was a lot like being a therapist: she made the guys feel good, and in the intimacy of the bedroom, they worked through a lot of their emotional hang-ups. She called it cathartic. Mostly, though, it was paying her way through grad school. Naturally enough, she was studying to be a psychologist.

"I'm going to lose him!"

"Reschedule."

"He's going out of town next week. Besides, you know what happens if you cancel the first time. It's over. And this guy…"

She got up, trailing the comforter, and went to her desk. "Look at him."

A few clicks on the keyboard later, a screen came up. A business site, with an executive profile. The photo showed him sitting behind a desk.

I gaped. "That's him?" Chiseled jawline, cheekbones to die for, thick, luxurious hair. His mouth was generous but tight, like he kept secrets he never shared. A touch of mystery, a hint of distance. And his suit jacket hung so well, it was obvious he was fit under those clothes.

"See why I'm bummed?"

"Why is he paying for sex? He could walk into a bar anywhere in the city and get ten women to follow him home. Like the Pied Piper of one-night stands."

"You'd be surprised at the men who pay for it. Sometimes they just want to be able to walk away after sex. Like you." She flashed me a smile. "It's less complicated when it's an up-front monetary transaction. Nobody's feelings get hurt. And Dylan sounded pretty intense. He's got baggage, clearly. Again, like you."

I ignored this last bit. No point in responding. Jeanine always claimed I should see a therapist about my relationship problem. I always told her I was fine the way I was, and my parents' deaths had nothing to do with who I was now, so why dig it up all over again? "You've talked to this Dylan?"

"Just email." She flopped back onto the bed, moving the handcuffs out of the way. "Too bad I don't have someone who could take my place. Unless..." She looked up at me from under long eyelashes. Coquettish.

I stared at her, dumbfounded. Me. In Jeanine's place. As a call girl.

She propped herself up on her elbows. "Oh my God, why didn't I think of it sooner? It's perfect."

"You're kidding, right?"

"You miss sex. Don't tell me you don't."

Her words caught at me, painful and true. Sex was being held, was spiraling into sensation. Sex was connection with another person, however dubious, however deceptive. Sex with an active, live partner was a whole lot better than a mechanical device. "Yes, but…"

"And yet you never go for it because it means being vulnerable to another human being, and you've never been comfortable with that. That's why your college relationships went belly-up."

I winced.

"Sorry, you know I love you, but it's true. But this time? You wouldn't even be you. You'd be me. Besides, Dylan isn't expecting a relationship. Just sex." She grinned, triumphant. "Perfect, like I said."

"As a call girl, though? It's not me. I'm not like you." A frisson of excitement shot through me, making my toes curl, belying my words.

"I'm sure you meant that as a compliment." She gave me a reproving look.

"Actually, yes. You've got balls. You get out there and take risks. I—" I gestured toward the door, where I'd left my leather bag from work. "I stay in and get work done. Which is fine. I love my job. But I'm not about to go and—"

"Why not? Do you find him unattractive?"

I hesitated. Unattractive? He was gorgeous. His chiseled looks, the intensity in his gaze… Yeah. I wanted to meet the man. But have sex with him? Well, yes, if I was honest with myself, that sounded amazing. Deliberate, planned-in-advance sex, though? Tonight?

Jeanine snorted. "Come on, Samantha, go for it for once in your life. He's a solid guy. Safe. One of my favorite clients referred him. I checked him out thoroughly, like always, but I'll give you a can of mace anyway."

"What if I do it wrong? What if he doesn't think I'm good in bed?"

She laughed. "I've seen you dance. You're the most sensual person I know, once you let yourself go. Trust your body. He'll love you."

"What if I didn't, you know…?" I gestured toward my crotch.

She rummaged in her bag and tossed me a tiny tube of lube. "You won't need it. You'll be sexed up and ready for action. Trust me. This guy is totally your type, and best of all, you get to walk away at the end of the night. He won't even have your phone number. You'll love it."

I held the lube between my fingers. The little tube made it feel so much more real. "I'm not you. Just because I worked at Greenpoint Pleasures for a few years doesn't mean I'm uninhibited and sex positive like you." Jeanine had helped me get the job at the feminist sex shop during college. It was the warmest, most wonderful workplace I'd ever had. Plus, I now had the world's biggest collection of dildos, thanks to my employee discount. "Anyway, I have piles of work to do, and you're talking about something that's happening tonight, no time to think it over." I set the lube down on the bed. It was almost invisible among the other sex toys. "I'm sorry. I wish I could help you." I could hear the quaver in my voice. The frisson of temptation.

Jeanine could too, apparently. "Are you sure?"

"I'm going to order from Szechuan Palace and get to work. Want anything?" I could feel the pulse beating in my throat, double-time. Me? Doing that? With him? Impossible. And yet...

I left Jeanine's room and went to get the takeout menu. Not that I needed it. I had the restaurant on speed dial, and the guy on the phone recognized my phone number from the caller ID. "Ms. Lilly, right? Chicken with broccoli and mu shu pork, same as usual?"

"Yes, that would be good. And a hot-and-sour soup. My roommate's got the flu."

"I hope she feels better soon. What show are you watching tonight?" Behind him, I heard the clatter of plates and a shout of laughter. People out on a Friday night, having a good time.

"I was thinking of mixing it up. Maybe watch a romantic comedy."

"Good to break up the routine. Your order will be there in forty-five minutes. Talk to you soon."

I returned the menu to the drawer, next to the pile of duck sauce packets and cheap wood chopsticks still sealed in their paper sheaths.

I'd sealed myself in a cocoon. Work, home, the occasional poker party with my old friends from Greenpoint Pleasures. All women. All safe. What was I so afraid of?

When I went into her room, Jeanine was reading a book under the comforter. On her desk, the computer was still on the same page. Dylan the hot executive. Maybe it was my imagination, but he looked hungry, in a good way. I pictured that gaze trained on me. I shivered with the feeling it engendered.

Maybe I could do this after all. I wouldn't know if I didn't try. Mixing it up for real.

Jeanine glanced up from her book. "What's up?"

"How would this work? If I said yes?"

Chapter Two

Two hours later, I strutted into the lobby of a Beaux Arts apartment building on the tony Upper West Side, clad in high-heeled boots and a whole pile of paper-thin courage.

Twenty minutes early. I should go to a coffee shop and wait, but the idea of waiting made me want to crawl out of my skin with anticipation mixed with fear in a heady, combustible stew.

I gave the security guy at the front desk my name. Well, Jeanine's name, or, rather, her work pseudonym. If Dylan Krause called me Saffron in the middle of an orgasm, would I know who he meant?

My mind skittered on the thought. That was what I was doing, going upstairs right now to give a guy an orgasm. Or two.

When I asked Jeanine a few months back if she enjoyed sex with her clients, she'd laughed and told me she almost always climaxed. She'd said there was something overpoweringly thrilling about being with someone that into what you're offering. And earlier tonight, as I was getting ready, she'd told me, *"Think of this as the best kind of one-night stand. Both of you know exactly what you're there for. Loosen up and have fun."*

The elevator had mirrored walls, so I got to see

myself in quadruplicate. Four-sided me, with cherry-red lips and loosely upswept hair, the dark wisps falling around my face. Jeanine had lined my eyes with a heavy stroke so I looked exotic, almost Egyptian. My peacoat hid my outfit: a tight red-and-black corset and a short flared skirt. No panties. A little surprise for my handsome client. I'd felt the wind lift my skirt briefly on the walk from the subway, giving me a thrill of chilly excitement, a reminder that yes, I was really doing this.

I was relieved to be alone in the elevator. Glad to have a moment to prepare myself for whatever was to come. Jeanine had assured me it would be fine. This was after saying yes had triggered my panic mode. *"You offer the whole Girlfriend Experience. I can't do that,"* I'd said. I couldn't be anyone's real girlfriend. How could I pretend that for someone I didn't even know?

Jeanine laughed, a delightful chortle. I could see why her clients adored her. "He doesn't want the GFE. This guy wants the wham-bam, thank-you-ma'am approach. No chitchat. Probably no talking at all. That's why it's so perfect for you. You get laid, and you don't even have to warm him up first."

She knew me too well. Small talk was my enemy. Never mind meeting a guy at a singles bar. I'd scare him away from me after drink number one. Too blunt, they always said, right after *"Oh my God, did you really say that?"*

Jeanine was right. I'd stay quiet, open my body, and have a good time. And in truth, there was something delicious about the mystery of it all. About playacting the part of a sexually experienced, physically confident professional escort.

The mirrored door opened. Fifteenth floor. Time to meet my client.

My heels clicked on the polished wood floor as I walked down the hallway, making me feel posh and sexy, like a siren from the movies.

His was the door at the end. I paused, took a deep breath, and rang the bell.

Footsteps. The door opened.

And there he was.

He was dressed in dark gray sweatpants with a plush red bathrobe loosely belted over it, and he was toweling his still-wet hair. Clearly, he'd just gotten out of the shower. A few droplets still shimmered in the cleft between his pecs.

"Saffron? I was expecting you later. But come on in." His deep baritone rumbled through me like a freight train.

Caught staring at his chest like a lascivious teenager, I quickly looked up at his face. And was immediately entranced by those full lips, those sculpted cheeks, and yes, that darkly hungry gaze, which was even stronger in person.

I obediently followed the sweep of his hand into the apartment. Hardwood floors, a simple but elegant crown molding, a picture rail. Prewar era, with at least some of the details intact, including a carved fireplace, which was, sadly, painted over.

The big windows had no covering at all, a stark frame for the dark-lit skyscrapers in Midtown. A plush, expensive modernist rug with circular patterns covered the center of the floor. There wasn't much furniture, just piles of moving boxes, a brown leather couch I could imagine sinking into, and a single curvaceous wood chair. A sensual one-of-a-kind piece, obviously handmade. It probably cost a fortune.

The daytime me, the architect Samantha Lilly, would love to get her hands on this place. The original apartment had obviously been cut up into smaller chunks at some point and never properly mended. It could be put right and made beautiful.

But tonight's version of me, Saffron the sex worker, was a different matter. She was all about the apartment's inhabitant.

I heard the door latch behind me with a quiet click as I turned toward Dylan, acutely aware I was now alone with a complete stranger who expected to have sex with me. An incredibly sexy stranger, but a stranger nevertheless.

Own it. I could hear Jeanine's words in my head. *Flaunt it.*

"So, uh…" He sounded as nervous as I felt. It gave me the courage I needed.

Flaunt it. Be your sexiest self. He has no idea who you are in real life. You will never see him again.

I unbuttoned my peacoat slowly, sliding each button out of the buttonhole and slipping my finger down to the next one. As I watched him watching me, I could see the rise of an erection under his sweatpants, see his eyes get even darker. We didn't have to know each other to know what we both wanted.

I could see why Jeanine liked her job.

Normally, I would have asked if I should hang the coat in the closet, or maybe draped it over the edge of the couch, but this wasn't me. This was Saffron. And Saffron made a statement with her every move.

I let the coat slip out of my fingers and pool onto the floor in an elegantly careless heap.

Dylan stared at me, openly appreciative.

My breasts jutted up under the thin fabric of the corset, eager for his touch. My skirt hid my bare bottom, but, I suspected, not for long. Not the way he was looking, like he wanted to suck the marrow from my bones.

So pure, this transaction. So simple. So insane.

"Like what you see?" I made my voice sultry, like

Mae West or what I imagined Jeanine to be like with a client. A mistake, because I immediately giggled at the absurdity.

Dylan raised his eyebrows. "Is this a joke to you?"

I walked over to him, a trifle unsteady on my stiletto boots but making it part of my sway, and pressed my hand against those damp curls on his chest. "Hardly a joke." I could feel his heart thump under my palm, nearly as fast as my own. "So? Do you want me to stay? Or do I refund your money?"

He was startled into a laugh. "Blunt. I like that."

"Good, because that's what you get. I'm all yours for tonight. Make use of me." I couldn't believe the words coming out of my mouth, but he seemed to like them.

"You're not what I expected." His gaze traveled over my body. I felt it like a caress.

I took another step, so close now, and ran my hand through his damp hair, enjoying the way it sprang against my fingers, a live thing. Enjoying the fact that I could do this. Hell, I could probably pull his sweats down right now and give him a blowjob, and he'd think it was part of the usual deal.

Except that probably wasn't how it was done. The client should lead, right? "What do you want to do first?"

He frowned. Was he having second thoughts? Was

he going to kick me out? After all that buildup, disappointment felt sharp in my throat.

But no. "This, I think." He ran a finger gently across my clavicle. My skin prickled.

His gaze followed his finger, his eyes hooded, his gaze remote.

He slipped one hand under the top edge of the corset and caressed my nipple with a rough thumb. "And this." The touch, skin to skin, so intimate and personal, made my body wake up with a jolt. Breath hissed through my teeth.

"Is that good?"

"Very." My breath stuttered. He'd know I wasn't faking anything.

"Who are you, Saffron?" He was looking at me with a strange, intent gaze.

This wasn't in the program. We were supposed to be having an impersonal encounter, a simple exchange of services. But I should be polite to the client. "What do you want to know?"

"For starters, how old are you?"

"Twenty-five. How old are *you*?" I let a challenging note sneak in. I was getting irritated.

But he merely looked amused. "Thirty-one. How long have you been a call girl?"

And here Jeanine had assured me he wouldn't want to talk.

"Long enough to know what I'm doing."

His fingers danced down my body across the lace and silk, over the flimsy skirt, down to my bare leg. Then up under my skirt. He was getting more comfortable with his role. He was also about to discover I wasn't wearing panties.

"Do you like the work?" His voice was husky. He was turned on. So was I.

Still, wasn't I supposed to be doing things to *him*? Things he'd paid good money to have done. Wasn't I supposed to be a body to him, not a person?

He looked at me. Intent. Like a predator. Waiting.

"I like sex." I felt embarrassed saying it, but it was apparently the right answer. He inhaled sharply.

Fingers sliding farther up my thigh, spreading shivers like a chain reaction. Fingertips reaching my groin, tangling in my pubic hair.

"Oh." I could hear the guttural surprise.

"Ohh." I groaned with pleasure as he curved those tantalizing fingers between my legs, flirted with my nerve endings, retreated. I was throbbing now, so hot for this man I knew nothing about.

Hot for him *because* I knew nothing about him.

Unexpectedly, he stepped away. He sat on the couch and rubbed his face. And yet he was clearly fully aroused, a powerful erection tenting his sweats.

"Do you want me to…?" I gestured toward it.

He laughed uncomfortably, and I knew. This was his first time paying for it.

The answers flooded in. An apartment filled with boxes. A man who clearly didn't need to pay for sex. Who was self-conscious about what we were doing.

I glanced down at his left hand. Sure enough, there was a lighter band of skin on his ring finger. A missing ring.

My chest tightened; a sympathetic nerve twanged. He might not be comfortable paying for sex, but for whatever reason, he needed this tonight. Needed me here.

I knelt in front of him. "May I?"

He nodded jerkily. I pulled his sweats down and off, leaving his bathrobe in place. There was something so sexy about a half-clad man, clean and ready for me. His erection jutted up expectantly, his arousal thick and strong. But he closed his eyes, pained. Not a sexy pain, not pleasure anticipated, though maybe some of that too. No, this was emotional. Like opening up unhealed wounds.

I paused. This wasn't right.

He opened his eyes. "Go ahead." But it sounded like *Go ahead and get this over with,* and that too was wrong.

I closed my hand around his cock, feeling it pulse against my palm. I spoke softly. "Dylan. I'm not only here because you hired me. I thought you should know. I find you incredibly attractive."

He opened his eyes. "You don't have to—"

I put my fingers to his lips. "When I saw your picture, I wanted you right then. Not just your body either. Something about you, it's…" I shook my head in wonderment, and I meant it. I didn't feel this way. Ever. But I did tonight. I wanted this. Wanted him. "I don't need to know your personal history. I don't need to know anything. But I thought you should know this. I'm here because I want to be."

It was the right thing to say. He let out his breath in a soft explosion of sound. "Thank you. I think I needed to hear that. It shouldn't matter, should it? But it does."

His cock jumped in my hand as I stroked the length, enjoying the feeling of supple skin, the ridge of aroused muscle beneath. He was going to feel so good inside me. He closed his eyes, and I could feel him finally start to give in to the experience.

My gaze strayed to the ghostly band on his ring finger. His ex must have done a number on him. I gradually sped up my strokes, listening to his breathing change and change again, feeling an answering quickening, a reflected pleasure at his response.

I'd never had sex with a man I didn't know. This was a first on so many levels. And yet it didn't feel like we were strangers anymore. Dylan was seminaked, his eyes slitted, his body open to me. It was all happening so quickly, and it felt so intense.

This could get addicting.

A Fountains of Wayne song abruptly started playing. Clearly a cell phone ringtone.

My hand spasmed. He pulled back.

"Sorry." I felt all sorts of cross with myself. Jeanine probably never let her concentration fade. "Do you need to…?" I gestured toward the ringing phone.

He shook his head. The phone stopped ringing, but the moment was gone. His erection was already fading.

What was the proper hooker etiquette here? Sympathy? Give him a breather? Work harder to turn him on?

Dylan made the decision first. He got up, cinched his bathrobe tight, and walked to the kitchen.

I stood in the living room, wearing a red-and-black corset, a short flirty skirt, and no panties. Not to mention the stiletto boots. It abruptly felt like the costume it was.

Dylan paused in the doorway to the kitchen. "Want something to drink?"

"Uh, sure." I sat on the couch and took my boots off, rubbing my feet. Stupid phone. I glared at it. As if in response, it beeped, signaling a voice mail.

Dylan came back into the living room with two wineglasses and a bottle of what looked like an expensive merlot, the kind with a discreet beige label written in French. He sat on the couch next to me and uncorked the bottle, then poured a little into the glasses, pulling the whole thing off with the panache of someone used to handling high-end wares. This was a man who knew what he wanted and paid for the best. The dense weave of the rug underfoot, the supple quality of the sofa's leather and solid workmanship of the wood frame. Not to mention the good bones of this apartment, which I would wager he owned.

I was struck once again by the strangeness of this self-contained man paying a call girl. But maybe that was why he had. Same as me. I was here because I didn't want to date. This was emphatically not a date, but rather a transaction. Need in exchange for need.

The phone rang again, the same tune. Dylan acknowledged the sound without comment as he handed me a glass. "Let it breathe a moment."

He swirled his wine. I copied him. The liquid licked up the sides of the glass and slid back down, deep red, jewellike. It smelled musky and fruity, redolent of forest and dry grasslands far from the city.

The phone stopped ringing. Dylan settled onto the couch, finally taking a sip.

I followed suit. The taste unfurled on my tongue.

"Why don't you turn it off?"

"I have to be reachable for work. Emergencies come up." He took another sip, contemplating the glass. "That was my wife. My ex-wife."

"Ah." I wasn't sure what else to say. *My condolences? Want a quick roll in the hay to help you forget?* "A recent divorce?"

"Four months last week. I found her in bed with my best friend." He contemplated the wine in his glass. "He's not my best friend anymore. And Persephone…"

"You don't have to tell me. It's okay. Honest."

He took a sip, steadying himself. I found myself watching his long fingers, his sure movements. "I didn't expect to tell you, but I'm glad I did. Maybe I need talk more than sex."

No sex? My face must have shown my dismay, because he caressed my exposed thigh, making his way up toward my groin. The touch both tickled and titillated.

"Okay, not more. Not after finding out how good you feel." He grinned, half mischievous little boy, half lascivious, entirely male—and slipped his finger inside me. The touch was so casually intimate, so possessive, so unexpected. It was a powerful aphrodisiac.

"I'll hold you to that promise, mister." I leaned in and kissed him. He looked surprised. Maybe I wasn't supposed to do that? But Jeanine hadn't given me any instructions about kissing, and I wanted it.

So did he, apparently. The kiss deepened quickly, tasting like wine and peppermint. He pushed me back against the couch, groaning into my mouth, his tongue against mine a delicious mimic of the full-on act. His hands covered my breasts, pinching the nipples hard through the fabric of my corset; his leg slid between my own, his engorged cock hard against my belly. I closed my hand around it and stroked him in time with the rhythm of our kiss.

His breathing got harsher against my mouth, his movements rougher. He slipped his hand under my skirt, tugging it up. I almost came up for air to tell him I had to fetch the condom, but Dylan surprised me, breaking the kiss and moving down my body. I could feel his fingernails through the satin sides of the corset, making me shiver. And then, yes, he flipped my skirt up, as I'd expected, but instead of his cock, I felt his mouth.

"I'm supposed to do that to you." It came out half-strangled. "I'm here for you."

"And what if this is what I want? I'll pay extra." His voice vibrated against my core. "You taste like lust." He flicked his tongue against me as he slid a finger inside. I clenched, a single involuntary spasm. Oh God. It had been so long since someone touched me like that. Caressed me, licked me, sucked me, breath and pressure and skill.

Without fully meaning to, I said it aloud.

Dylan lifted his head but thankfully didn't stop moving his thumb and fingers. "It has? You?" He licked me in one long stroke, back to front.

"Y-yes." I shuddered on an exhale.

"Tell me." It was a command.

"I shouldn't. It's unprofessional and—"

He pulled back. "Tell me." The implicit threat: *I'll stop doing this amazing thing to you.*

Maybe this was part of the service an escort was supposed to provide? If the client asks, answer? I'd have to question Jeanine when I got home. But right now, my body was thinking for me, and it was saying, *want more, want now.*

I lifted my head, looked into his dark, hungry eyes, and got lost. "I gave up sex—I mean recreational sex—a couple of years ago."

"Why? Do you dislike it?" His tone was carefully neutral, but I knew I'd lose all the trust I'd gained if I said the wrong thing.

"I love it." My body throbbed with his ministrations. Yes. I loved it. Loved *this.* "But I tried having a boyfriend in college a couple of times. Bad idea. I'm not programmed for it. They wanted things I couldn't give them." Intimacy. Promises. Saying I loved them when I didn't—when I couldn't. "So that left me with one-night stands. But they're all groping and awkwardness, you know? Or maybe you don't. And some of the guys, they think we're starting a relationship. And—"

"You're not programmed for it."

"Which makes it even more awkward."

"So you do this instead."

I sat up and grabbed him by his shoulders, pushing down his red bathrobe. "Enough talking. Isn't it time for this to come off?" One yank on the belt, and the plush robe dropped to the floor. I gave him a sweeping gaze, head to toe and oh, the male real estate in between. This man was in good shape: sculpted muscles, taut abdomen, and that thick, sexy cock jutting out like a divining rod.

"That's more like it." I bit his neck gently, then licked his chest, nibbling my way down the narrow line of hair that was like an arrow pointing the way south. Follow the directions to the Candyland Pleasure Palace.

"You're still dressed."

I paused. "You want me to change that?"

"Eventually."

I licked and sucked my way farther down, spreading my hands across his muscled body, enjoying the curves and ridges, until I reached his pelvis. As he arched up and I took the silken tip of his cock into my mouth, the phone rang. The same ringtone song.

Of course it did.

Dylan met my gaze. Shook his head. I took that as a signal to keep going, so I did. Licked up the underside of his cock to the ring of a progressive rock song, trying to ignore his tension. Licked the base as the ringing stopped. Licked up again, my hand cupping his balls. I could feel him relax into the silence, breathe into the charged air. Felt him turn sexy again.

The phone rang yet again.

Chapter Three

"For heaven's sake!" Dylan jumped up, stark naked, and stalked over to where his cell phone rested on a pile of moving boxes. His jutting cock bounced with every stride. At least he was still turned on. He picked up the phone. "Enough! Stop calling me!"

I could hear the woman on the other end. Her tone was apologetic, but she kept talking. And talking.

Dylan rubbed his forehead. "The paperwork? Call my lawyer. Don't call me."

She said more. He sat on the couch. Stress lines turned his mouth down. He radiated tension.

I picked up my forgotten glass of wine and took a big gulp to steady my nerves, wishing for something stronger, something that would burn on the way down. What a disaster.

I put the glass down and scooped up my peacoat from the floor.

Dylan put his hand over the mouthpiece. "What are you doing?"

"I think I should go." I was proud of myself; my voice didn't quiver. I'd slam my fist into my pillow later and stomp around my room in a dazed rage, wondering why the hell something as straightforward as this got so screwed up. Right now, though, I was going to hold it together. This encounter might have turned as flaccid as Dylan's cock, but dammit, I was going to walk away with my dignity intact. Or as intact as it could be in this ridiculous seduction costume.

"Don't go." His gaze sliced through me like a longing I'd only ever felt in echoes before. Into the phone, he said, "Persephone, we'll finish this conversation later. But not now." She obviously asked about me, because he said, "Nobody you know."

This was apparently a trigger. Her voice got louder, becoming a wail.

"Persephone. We're getting a divorce. You know that means we're going to see other people." He raked his free hand through his hair, his head bent so I could see the nape of his neck. "No. I can't—please stop crying. You have to let go of this. Of me."

I looked longingly at my peacoat. This was getting messy. I wanted nothing more than to make my escape, and fast.

But then there was Dylan, sitting on the couch. Completely, beautifully naked, an artist's wet dream— but so taut, so tense. The tendons in his neck bulged; his hands were clenched. His body was wound up like a top, about to spin out of control.

I had a choice. Go home and minister to my aching need with my pink vibrator, or make this work.

Earn my money. Make Dylan hang up the phone.

He'd obviously made an appointment with Saffron because he needed to heal from something entirely too toxic. And here was Ms. Toxic.

Time to be assertive. Take control of the situation, not let it unravel and leave both of us suffering the backwash of one woman's self-inflicted pain.

I let the peacoat drop onto the arm of the couch. Turning around to face away from him, I unzipped my skirt, letting it fall on the polished parquet floor. I rummaged for a moment in my coat pocket, and then finally I turned back toward him.

I knew what I looked like. I'd checked myself out in the mirror before I put the skirt on. Clad in a silk-and-lace corset that skirted my pubic bone. And then nothing but groin and leg until my calf-hugging leather stiletto boots. I was dressed like a goddamned fantasy centerfold, and I was going to use it.

So yes, I turned back toward him, exquisitely slowly. His gaze was locked to my body. He breathed shallowly through his mouth. He was fully erect again. A different man from a moment ago. Transformed.

But he still spoke into the phone. "It might be good for a few months, sure, but what about when you get restless again?"

He was far too controlled. I wanted to break that control.

I reached behind my back and pulled the laces on my corset, loosening it. Held my breasts from underneath, plumping them up.

He hissed softly through his teeth.

My breasts came free, and the corset fell open.

"Persephone. I'm going *right now*. Don't call again tonight. Call a therapist. Figure out why you keep committing adultery. But don't call me."

He hung up.

Now it was the two of us. I wasn't a distraction. I was the main event. And I was in the middle of a striptease? What was I thinking?

I faltered.

"Don't stop. Keep doing that." Dylan's gaze was intent, his tone authoritative.

Swallowing hard, I spread my legs, a wide stance, and ran my hands slowly down my body. The corset fell to the floor. I was naked except for my boots. And then I touched myself.

It was like and not like doing it at home. The movements, the feel of my fingers, that was the same. But at home, I closed my eyes and pretended I was with a virile man. Pretended he wanted to devour me whole.

Now? I watched an extremely sexy man closely, watched as his eyes lit with hunger. Watched his hand tighten around his cock. Heard his breath thicken.

I strode over to him, feeling powerful. Excitement zinged through me. I straddled his lap. He looked ready. I sure was. I took the condom I'd palmed a minute earlier, ripped it with my teeth.

I cocked an eyebrow—a question. He held his breath—an answer.

Unfurling the condom was another game. Another chance to touch him, to caress him. His cock at full attention, thick and strong, and oh man, that was going to feel amazing inside me.

I slid on top of him, against him, and finally, yes, took him inside me. He filled me, the tension unbearable.

I raised myself up, letting him slip partway out.

The phone rang.

"God. Don't stop." Dylan wrapped his hands around my hips, urging me on.

I slid back down, embedding him deep inside me as I grabbed the phone. "I'm going to answer it."

He stared up at me, his face a wild mix of passion and shock. But he didn't say no.

I thumbed the slider. "Persephone, sweetheart. I'm fucking your ex-husband. Find yourself someone else to screw up. He's not available."

I hung up on her choked gasp and threw the phone across the room. It clattered against some boxes.

"I can't believe you did that." But he wasn't angry.

He was turned on. "My God."

I lifted myself up until he was barely inside me, and then slid back down, taking him all the way in. He groaned and flipped us around, pinning me to the couch.

He was laughing, relief and passion and a pure, piercing joy. I vibrated with his joy, with his laughter, and all the while he was plunging into me, making me moan in pleasure.

"You."

He thrust, sending sensation cascading through me.

"Are."

Again, and so good.

"Insane."

I laughed and wrapped my legs around him, urging him on, boot leather against flesh. And he obliged. Oh, how he obliged. Laughing and groaning and panting and surging into me as I reared up to meet him. I kept my eyes open, watching pleasure tighten his stunning features, watching what I was doing to him. And he opened his eyes, gazing at me with a deep well of hunger and delight.

We moved faster, in perfect sync. I'd never been so in tune with a man in my life, with this stranger who was anything but. My body surrounded him, moved against him. We moved in rhythm as if we'd known each other forever, as if this night was kismet, meant to be. Perfectly insane. Insanely perfect.

I could hardly breathe from the pleasure coursing through my veins, every pore of my skin sexually charged.

He lifted me up, still joined, and walked us to the bedroom, where he set me down on a huge king-size bed. I rolled us around so I was on top again. With him still inside me, I unfastened my barrette. As my hair spilled out of its confinement, I leaned forward, letting it brush across his bare chest. The tingling got stronger, a wave of pressure building inside me, until I was about to burst. I wanted to bring him with me, so I reached down and fingered his testicles and rode him, slick and hard, until we both exploded, his pulsing merged into mine, and then I brushed my breasts against his chest, kissed him on the lips, and collapsed on him.

And it was all far, far better than I'd imagined. I felt free. No relationship drama. No complications looming. No *I love you* and freeze. Just a deliciously pleasurable intimate connection with an unexpectedly fascinating man.

Dylan murmured something into my hair. I rolled over to lie next to him, wanting to see him better. We hadn't even gotten under the sheets. He brushed my hair out of my face, a surprisingly tender gesture.

"Saffron. Spicy. Exotic."

"Mmm."

"What's your real name?"

Panic pinged through me. But I shook my head with a saucy smile. "Saffron, of course."

He laughed. A long way from the tightly wound man I'd met at the door.

I too felt boneless and wide open. Just not open enough to tell him the truth. "Gotta keep some secrets, don't I?"

He traced the line of my cheek. "I want to do that again in a bit."

I propped myself up on my elbows. "You want your ex to call so we can reenact the drama? A bit excessive, don't you think?"

Now his finger traced loops across my chest. And yes, I felt stirrings of lust reemerge. Light from the night-bright city slanted across his face, revealing a look more tender than hungry. "I still can't believe you did that."

"Which? The striptease or answering the phone? I'm not one for social niceties."

He laughed. "I kind of got that." He leaned in for a kiss, first gentle and then more hungry. When we broke apart, he leaned back against the pillow. "I needed it, though. I won't be able to listen to her on the phone again without thinking about this." He gestured between us. "And then I'll probably get horny. Do you have discounts for regular customers?"

"We'll see." I smiled in the dark, but I could feel my stomach clench. Regular customers? I knew Jeanine did that, but if I came back here, if I saw him again—it was treading dangerously close to a relationship.

I sat up. "Why think about the future? Why not work with what we have?" I brushed my hand lightly down his body, my mouth following suit.

Yep, he had an erection. Juicy and full and eager for my touch, my tongue, my heat.

This time I bent over the end of the bed, and he entered me from behind. I squeezed my thighs together and reached my hand down to touch the base of his cock, feeling every movement both within and without.

He withdrew, but only to roll me onto the bed and enter me from above. His arms were taut as he drove into me with an ever-increasing rhythm, the bed shaking with the force of our joining. When I came, I felt my throat clog with unshed tears, and I didn't know why.

After a few boneless moments, I got up and went to the bathroom, where I ran his comb through my hair and tried to make myself presentable. My hair was mussed, my cheeks pink from exertion, and half my makeup had rubbed off. I looked like a different person. Like someone well satisfied.

I hesitated before crossing the threshold back into the bedroom. Dylan leaned back against the pillows, watching me. The tension that had propelled him earlier was gone, but he didn't look as relaxed as I would have expected. He looked alert. Focused.

I walked into the room cautiously, acutely aware of his gaze. We'd been so intimate, and now…well, now here we were. This was the hard part. The part where things always got awkward. For one thing, I had no idea what to say. *That was great, thanks?*

He spoke first. "Who hurt you?"

"Excuse me?"

"You said you're not programmed for relationships. Why not? Who hurt you?"

"Nobody hurt me." *Not on purpose, anyway.*

"Tell me the truth."

"True confessions cost extra."

"I'll pay."

I was tempted to brush him off again with a quip. It would be so much easier. But then I remembered watching Dylan on the phone, taut and tense. Remembered the look on his face when I first touched him intimately, how it wasn't only pleasure for him. He'd been guarded and tense, anticipating pain.

Remembered his expression when I left him on

the bed two minutes ago, relaxed against the pillows, like a male model, radiating contentment.

He'd shared his pain with me. Thanks to Persephone and her incessant phone calls, he hadn't had a choice. The least I could do was return the favor.

So, for the first time in my life, I didn't run away. Instead, I sat on the end of the bed and draped a sheet over my bare lap, feeling acutely self-conscious. "It wasn't on purpose. My parents—my father died of a heart attack when I was seven. My mother went to bed and did nothing but cry for two years. He'd been her entire life. With him gone, she became practically catatonic. So my grandparents, my mother's parents, they took me in. And then after she committed suicide, they kept me until I graduated high school. They were…" I misted over, remembering, then angrily rubbed my eyes. No crying allowed. Not ever. "They were crotchety and old-fashioned and had stupid rules that drove me crazy."

He watched me, his eyes dark with something dangerously like understanding. "And you loved them."

"I had to. They were all I had."

"Are they still around?"

"My grandfather is. We talk twice a year. I call him on his birthday, and he calls me on mine."

"Thank you for telling me." He sounded like

maybe *he* was about to cry. He sat up so he could stroke my back. I leaned into it like a cat arching into a soothing hand, then shifted my body against his and turned around to slither into his lap.

This time we took it slow. He moved with great care and held me as if I might break. My orgasm ratcheted up gradually, like steam building in a teakettle instead of a tidal wave, but when it hit, it lasted for an incredibly long time. I opened my eyes and stared up into his deep brown gaze, and wished I could stay here forever, in this moment, in this bed, with this man, in suspended animation, this perfect moment with light from the city night streaming over us and the soft sheets and his hard abs and everything about tonight captured in this one embrace.

Afterward, while Dylan cleaned up in the bathroom, I fell asleep, boneless and exhausted. I woke when I felt the weight of his body as he got back into bed, and I struggled against the lure of sleep, forcing myself to sit up. "I should go. What time is it?"

"Three a.m. You might as well stay."

I hesitated. This was starting to feel an awful lot like a date.

"I'll pay the extra cost, if that's your concern."

Now I felt bad. "That's not why."

He leaned forward, brushing the hair from my face. His expression was too knowing. "You don't sleep over, do you? It's in your price chart, but you don't ever do it."

Too personal. He knew too much. I rolled away from him on the bed, searching for my clothes, before I realized I'd left them in the living room.

He followed me from the bedroom. I picked up my corset. I couldn't face putting it back on, so I grabbed my coat from the couch. With the coat buttoned securely, I could fake my way into a cab. I'd bring the corset with me.

Dylan watched me. "You and I are alike in some ways, I think."

I paused, one arm through a sleeve, the other bare. "How so?"

"You build walls around yourself. Protective."

I turned toward him. "You seem like the opposite to me. You've been kind to your ex even after what she did to you." *And you were more than kind to me.* His touch, his mouth. Giving, not only receiving.

His mouth quirked up. "Learned behavior. Persephone acts so fragile, it would be like kicking a puppy."

I slid my other arm into the sleeve but let the coat hang open, my nudity half-concealed. "Are you saying I was cruel to her on the phone?" Maybe I'd taken it too far. I didn't know her, didn't know their relationship.

"You know you were."

"Then why do you want me to stay?"

A small smile played across his face, almost mischievous. "I didn't say it was wrong for you to be cruel. I can't say the things you did. We have too much history. But someone should tell her she needs to move on, and tell her emphatically."

I sat on the couch, sucked in despite myself. "That wasn't the first time she slept with someone else, I take it." I couldn't exactly walk out on Dylan. Not with him standing there, his nude body sculpted by light, showing every supple muscle, the tension rippling through him.

"She's a serial adulterer. She craves the excitement. Whenever I'd catch her, she'd deny it, then burst into tears and swear she loved me, only me, and beg forgiveness." He heaved a sigh and sat on the couch. The leather squeaked, and I could feel the cushion rebalance with his weight. "I knew she'd do it again, every time. But she was like a wounded bird. I thought I could fix her and make it all better."

"But it hurt. Her adultery."

His silence was assent, heavy in the air.

"Is this the first time you moved out?"

He nodded. "The first time I've slept alone for more than a night or two. We were together for twelve years. No children, thankfully. We met freshman year of college. She was family. And now she's not." He ran his palm along the slick leather surface between us. "I don't sleep well here. It's not home yet."

A truck backfired several floors down, out in the street. The wind rattled the windowpanes. "I'll stay tonight."

"Good." He got up and went into the kitchen. I followed, still wearing the coat, feeling awkward and uncertain. This was no longer anything like a sex-for-pay encounter, but it also wasn't a date. Without a label, without that definition of purpose, I didn't feel right stripping off the coat and being naked with him. The coat was my defense. Feeble as that simple wool layer might be, it was symbolic.

The refrigerator door was open, spilling light onto Dylan's nude form. I admired his silhouette, the outlines of his buttocks, the dimple in the small of his back. One fine man, for sure. He turned around, and I could see the plate he held, neatly arranged with pâté, a jar of fish roe, and a wedge of cheese.

"I can cut an apple." I grabbed one from the fruit bowl and looked around for a knife.

Dylan handed it to me, then peeled the coat off, letting it drop, and pulled me against him. So much for symbolism. Or maybe that *was* the symbolism. This man wouldn't let me have my shields. I could handle that for tonight. I'd never see him again, after all, so why not? So I cut the apple in neat slices while standing naked with a naked man pressed against my backside. It was wildly erotic but also strangely right.

We ate sitting cross-legged on his huge bed, the plate between us on the coverlet. I fell on the food, ravenous. I'd skipped dinner. The butterflies in my stomach hadn't allowed for food.

Dylan cut a slice of cheddar and laid it neatly on an apple slice. His gaze flicked up to my mouth. I could tell he was thinking about feeding me by hand. I grabbed an olive and stuffed it in my mouth. If he fed me, it would feel too intimate. Too much like love.

He ate the apple-cheese combination himself in one bite and washed it down with a sip of wine. "So why a call girl?"

I froze, the next olive halfway to my mouth. But Dylan was focused on the cracker he was now spreading with a generous dollop of pâté, as if it was the most natural question in the world. After the events of the night, maybe it was.

"It's a good living. I meet the most interesting people." I flashed him a smile and slid my hand along the lightly furred muscle of his thigh.

He responded instantly, sighing under my touch, but apparently it didn't distract him enough. "It's not exactly a long-term career path. You're obviously intelligent. Ingenious too." His mouth twitched. I'd done some interesting things tonight, hadn't I? "So why not grad school? Become, I don't know, a lawyer. Or a surgeon. You're good with your hands." He gave me a sidelong look, and I blushed. "It's not too late. You're young."

He looked so earnest. I almost blurted out that I was a junior architect at a good firm, but that would not only give the game away, it wasn't fair to Jeanine. She deserved better. Her work-for-pay gig deserved better.

And it wasn't Dylan's fault he didn't get it. Most people didn't. "It's only a problematic employment choice if you think sex is dirty. Think of it as a service profession. Giving to people. Helping them. Like I helped you start to get over your ex tonight. Sometimes it means giving clients something they can't have otherwise. Companionship, or a satisfying roll in the hay after a long drought. Or kink, if they want that and can't find it anywhere else. Or just a simple release."

He took a bite of pâté-smeared cracker, chewing as if it tasted bad, which I knew it didn't. "Don't you ever want it to mean more, though? I know you're not into having a boyfriend, but what if you did? How would you keep doing this and have someone serious in your life? How would you differentiate sex with him versus sex with clients?"

"You're overthinking this." I pushed the plate aside and put my hand on his thigh. He didn't protest, but I felt his tension, and not the good kind. "I love what we did earlier. There was something so pure about it. I walked in here knowing I was going to feel you inside me, and that was such an amazing thing. No 'I'll buy the lady a drink, what's your name, pretty girl?' bullshit."

He choked with laughter. "I never do that."

"I'm sure you're much smoother. Still, the point is, it makes it simple, doesn't it? We both knew we'd get laid tonight from the moment I walked in that door. I like you, and I enjoy talking to you more than I expected." My throat closed at this, and I didn't know why. "But we didn't have to talk at all. Purely optional. Bodies, that's all we need to connect."

I brushed my fingers lightly against his cock. Unbelievably, it stirred under my touch, though not to fullness. Even after all the times we'd brought each other to orgasm tonight, he was still turned on by my light caress. The thought was intoxicating. That intoxication stirred something inside of me too, an answering kindling, albeit a muted one after our long night together.

We rolled over to the other side of the king-size bed and explored each other's bodies. I marveled at the slide of skin on skin, at the ripples of his muscles, the way they bunched and clenched. We fooled around but weren't up for much more. It was about touch and wordless contact.

I ended up nestled into the curve of Dylan's arms, my ear against his chest, lulled by the steady rhythm of his heartbeat. I told myself I'd get up as soon as he fell asleep. It was morning now, the sky growing lighter by the minute, and the last thing I wanted was toast and bacon with this man. With any man. It was far too cozy.

But I must have fallen asleep, because the next thing I knew, his phone was ringing with a non-Persephone ringtone, my bladder was full, and the sun was way too bright.

As I sat up, Dylan picked up the phone and started talking about mergers and office space, saying he'd stop by on Monday. His voice sounded so different from the way it had during our night-dark confidences. His tone now was that of a polished executive in a suit and tie, for all he looked delectably naked and rumpled, the sheets a tangled swirl around his knees.

I got up to use the bathroom. When I came out, he stood, skated his fingers playfully along my bare shoulders, and went into the bathroom, all while still on the phone.

If I waited for him to get off the phone, we'd

probably have sex again. My groin throbbed, a pleasant ache, but I'd ridden and been ridden and was ready for a hot bath and a long nap. Still, another round with Dylan would be worth it.

But if I stayed into the morning, that glint in his eye and the way he stroked my skin as he went past, they said this thing between us would turn into something more. It felt like it already had. And that wasn't okay.

My heart thumping, I grabbed one of his T-shirts from the dresser and threw it on, then retreated to the living room, scooped up my skirt and boots, and rescued my coat from the kitchen floor. Then I fled.

When I got outside, I gazed up. The second floor from the top, over on the right side. His living room windows. I raised my hand in a half salute. *Good-bye, Dylan. It was amazing being with you.*

Chapter Four

I'd planned to slip quietly past the presumably ailing Jeanine's bedroom and make it to the privacy of my own room without telling her anything. Oh, I would eventually, but not yet, not until I'd had a chance to process it myself. But she wasn't lounging in her bedroom on her computer, nor was she taking one of her hour-long scaldingly hot baths. Or, for that matter, sleeping off her flu in bed.

Nope. She was perched on the couch facing the door, remarkably healthy.

"Look who finally showed up." Jeanine smirked at me. "It was fun, right? Can I say 'told you so'?"

I growled at her and walked past into my bedroom and privacy. Or, rather, I tried. She leapt up from the sofa and followed me in. "Nuh-uh, you don't get to walk away. Spill. I've been dying since that tantalizing text you sent me at some crazy hour saying that you were spending the night."

"You seem awfully perky for someone who was moaning under your comforter yesterday. Don't you have to go lie down? Being sick and all." I took the coat off and hung it up.

"Good immune system. I bounced back quick." She gaped at my attire—Dylan's tee engulfing my torso, a stark contrast to my provocative skirt. "What happened to the corset?"

"Left it behind. Won't be needing it again anyway."

"That was mine!"

Right. I knew that. I was so tired this morning, I wasn't thinking straight. "Buy you a new one?" I sat on the bed to unzip my boots.

"I'll let it go if you tell me everything. You had sex, obviously. Was it great? Did you like being me? Did you do naughty things to him? Was he as hot as his picture?"

"It was pretty good. I had an okay time." I tried to keep a straight face.

"Not getting out of it that easy. Tell all. And I mean *all*."

I let the boots drop to the floor and flopped back on the bed. It felt good to rest. My groin gently ached, a pleasant reminder. "Okay, yes, he was hot. He was wearing a bathrobe when I got there, and I thought about climbing him like a mountain, licking him like a lollipop, and humping him like we were billy goats in heat. And we pretty much did all three by the end of the night. That good enough for you?"

Jeanine looked only slightly mollified. But that was all she was getting. I yawned and closed my eyes, reliving the moment I walked into that apartment. The drop of water glistening on his chest. The look on his face, hunger mixed with pleased recognition.

I sat up abruptly. "You planned it, didn't you?" I jumped up off the bed and made for the door.

Jeanine stepped back out of my way as I barreled past, and then followed me across the hall. "I was sick. I'm much better today."

I paused in her doorway. "And what about the picture? Don't you send your prospective clients a photo of yourself? He recognized me. From your photo. Which makes sense. Because we *look so much alike*." I stared at her dusky Indian complexion, the luxurious black hair that fell to the small of her back, her oval Modigliani face, and her turned-up nose. My hair was reddish brown and shoulder length, my nose was straight, and my face was more triangular. Heart-shaped, my father had called it.

I plopped down in her desk chair and turned on her computer.

"Hey, that's mine. You can't—"

"And my life is mine. And yet..." I arched an eyebrow at her, daring her to stop me. "I want to see the picture you sent him."

"Fine. I'll show you." She made shooing gestures.

I got up. She sat in my place and quickly pulled up the message with, yup, a photo of me smiling into the camera, taken last summer on the High Line. Hard to believe she used it as a come-hither shot for a call-girl gig. Sure, I was wearing a hot-pink tank top, but I was hardly seductive, with my hair blowing across my mouth and into my eyes while I finished off an ice-cream cone. "You used *that* picture?"

She grinned. "You look adorable. All mussed up, like you just got out of bed. And the ice cream is very suggestive."

I almost laughed with her, but then I remembered I was still mad. "Why did you do it? Why set me up like that? That was a crap thing to do."

Jeanine swiveled her chair around to face me. "Was it?" She gave me a once-over, and I was suddenly aware of my disheveled, satiated condition, not to mention the huge black T-shirt I'd filched from Dylan, emblazoned with an image of Animal, the wild drummer from *The Muppet Show.*

"You should have asked. You should have included me."

"And you'd have said no. Like you say no every time some guy invites you out for a drink, like you say no every time we're invited to some big party where there are lots of hot guys. Come on, Sam. You and I both know you needed a kick in the pants."

I folded my arms across my chest, protective. "Is there something wrong with wanting to be alone?"

"You don't want that, though. You're just afraid to

put yourself out there."

"So you did it *for* me?"

"That's what friends do. They help their friends. I did it because I love you, dammit! And because you needed to get laid. To loosen up about the act without worrying about what comes after. I just got rid of the hard part for you—the dating dance."

"You think that's the only hard part?"

Her gaze sharpened. "What happened? Did he do something inappropriate? Did he hurt you?"

"God, no. He was an incredible lover. Considerate, passionate. Sexy." I inhaled, remembering. "But you know the part where he didn't want a GFE? Where this would be a simple sexual encounter, leave your feelings at the door? Not so much."

She leaned forward, compassion in her eyes. "Tell me."

So I did. And it felt good, replaying the night in detail, leaving out little. This was Jeanine, after all. She talked sexual positions as if she was recounting dinner at an exclusive restaurant, with zero embarrassment. But even her eyes widened when I described my striptease while Dylan was on the phone. She whistled and clapped. "You go, woman! Awesome."

"It wasn't like that. It was…" I shook my head. I had felt so many things, how could I sum it all up?

I thought about Jeanine, about her relationships

with her clients. About some of the questions Dylan had asked. "Do you ever think about giving up the life?"

"And pay for grad school how? Go into massive debt like the rest of my classmates? No thanks."

I was about to push her, but her email chimed with an incoming message. She swiveled toward the screen. "It's from Lover Boy."

"Which one?"

"Yours. Dylan Krause."

The jolt I felt at his name was entirely unexpected. The flush more so. Damn. He was just a one-night lay. What was wrong with me?

"What did he say?"

"Read it."

I leaned forward, cursing my eagerness.

Sorry you left so fast. I was looking forward to breakfast, or rather, lunch. You're pretty amazing. Best therapy ever. I'm still smiling as I look at the corset. Which, by the way, doesn't fit me. If you give me your address, I'll mail it to you. Unless you want to pick it up in person? Maybe try it on again?

Dylan

I shivered, hearing the words in his deep voice, the memory thrumming through me.

See him again?

Jeanine gave me a sidelong smile. "Want to set up

a return engagement? Maybe you can get another T-shirt out of the deal."

I almost said yes. The sex was so good, and I'd still be Saffron, not Samantha. He'd pay me. An exchange of services.

Yeah, right. After last night, did I seriously think Dylan would keep a safe emotional distance? That he wouldn't ask me a million personal questions, that he wouldn't share intimacy like it was a gift rather than a ticking time bomb?

If I walked into that spookily beautiful empty apartment today or next week or even next month, he'd greet me like an old friend. No, an old lover. We now had a past, he and I. Shared intimacy. And if I went back, we'd share more. We'd build a relationship.

And I couldn't risk my heart. Not for him, not for anyone.

"Once was enough. Write him back, say thanks for the night. It was fun."

I made myself turn around and leave Jeanine's room, closing the door behind me.

Chapter Five

Dylan, it turned out, wasn't the kind of guy to give up easily. He must have had as good a time together as I had. He'd emailed back and forth with Saffron a dozen times that first week. He asked where to mail the corset. *It's okay, I don't need it.* Asked where to send flowers. *Sweet thought, but you won't get my address that way, sneaky man.* And then he got to the real point and asked when he could see me again. Said he'd pay for a night, an overnight, a weekend. He was exuberantly extravagant at first, and Jeanine kept gazing at me with sad eyes over her breakfast oatmeal, asking when I'd finally say yes, because I obviously wanted to.

Though Saffron was kind and warm and even a little flirty at times, her schedule was crazy busy. She wasn't sure when she could fit him in, but she'd let him know. Then she was laid up in bed with a bad flu. If it worked for Jeanine, why not me? And then I—or rather, she—said she couldn't see him again. That it was too close to a real date.

Yeah, a little bit of truth crept in there, despite my best intentions.

Then he stopped emailing. And that felt worse.

The first month, I told myself I could live on the memories and my handy-dandy vibrator.

The second month, I stopped by Greenpoint Pleasures on my way home to pick up another vibrator. My old one was obviously faulty.

The third month, I tossed the new vibrator. It buzzed louder than the ancient window air conditioner keeping my room semicool in the midsummer heat wave. Mostly, it wasn't the same as the real thing.

The fourth month, I leaned over the divider at work and asked Rudy if he had time for a quick lunch. Anything to distract me. To remind me there were other men. We sat at a plastic booth in a pizza joint around the corner and munched on calzones. Rudy was charming and funny, and I felt nothing for him. We did have lunch again a couple of weeks later, though.

The fifth month, I told Jeanine I was taking a vow of celibacy. She laughed. I smacked her with a pillow.

Now, six months after the most intimate night of my life, I sat at my drafting table in the large main office at Alvarez and Associates and tried to work on a remodel of a Greenwich Village brownstone, but my mind kept wandering. It had been exactly six months. To the day. May 15th to October 15th. Dylan had undoubtedly moved on. I should too.

I bent back to my work. Let's see, if we removed the wall between the living and dining room, we'd have to add a couple of columns to maintain the structural integrity…

A voice rumbled through me. It came from behind me. Was it my imagination? The fact that I'd been thinking of him? It had to be. What would Dylan Krause be doing here? And why on earth would he be saying, "We'd have to examine the costs of building from scratch versus renovating the sales floor"? Clearly, I was mishearing the Juniper Designs guy Fernando was meeting with this afternoon while dreaming of that amazing night six months ago.

Still, I turned around on my stool to check. Even while I scolded myself, I turned around. And couldn't breathe.

It was Dylan. Far too handsome in a slim-cut dark blazer and a pale blue shirt, no tie. Clean-shaven. Hair only a tiny bit mussed. Rock-star hot. *Here.*

I hastily turned back to my drafting table. Maybe he hadn't spotted me. He'd been focused on my boss as they walked together down the aisle toward the corner office. I gripped my pencil so hard, it snapped in two. Another second and he'd be safely past me.

No such luck. I felt his sudden looming presence by my table. "Saffron?" He sounded incredulous.

Compelled, I looked up into those dark eyes. Hungry? He looked ravenous. And something else, something I hadn't seen that night: a quiet fury, tightly leashed.

Fernando was right behind him. And if Dylan was the client, then damn. Because Fernando had been talking all week in meetings about how big this fish was, how important it was that we land this account. If I screwed it up by being Saffron at the wrong time…

I stuck out my hand. "Samantha Lilly. Nice to meet you, Mr…?"

He wasn't fooled, not for a second. "You work here?"

"So it would appear." I tried for light, casual. Puzzled, even.

Fernando was frowning. "What's going on, Sam?"

"I'm not sure." I turned back to Dylan, cocking my head. "Oh, wait, I think I remember you. Didn't we meet at the Steiners' cocktail party, back in May?"

Please, Dylan, take the hint.

He did. "That's right. I'm sorry, I guess I forgot your name." I could see his fists clenched by his sides and the twitch in his cheek, but, with luck, Fernando couldn't.

Dylan turned to Fernando. "I'm sorry, do you mind if we delay our meeting a few minutes? There's something I'd like to ask your colleague."

Fernando looked baffled but nodded.

Dylan grabbed my arm. "We need to talk."

I got up. He kept his grip firm, as if he thought I

might bolt.

I glanced back over my shoulder at Fernando. "It's the Steiners. Their situation is complicated. Big fight. Disaster of a party."

My last glimpse of him as we walked away was a furrowed brow. Fernando wasn't a dumb guy, even if he was a little stuffy. I'd have to come up with something more plausible later. But right now Dylan was holding my arm, and I had to find a place we could talk where my sexploits wouldn't be broadcast through the entire office in a matter of minutes.

Marie's office. She'd gone out on maternity leave two weeks ago. She had an office with a door that closed and no window glass. Completely private. I led Dylan there through the familiar warren of computer workstations and drafting tables, trying not to think about what this all meant, what Dylan would say. Trying to ignore the frisson of pleasure that snaked through me at the thought that he was here, walking mere steps behind me, his footsteps hard on the cement floor.

Once safely inside Marie's office, I locked the door and heaved a sigh of relief. Dylan turned to me, his face a mask. He thrust his hand out. "Dylan Krause. And you are…?"

I ignored it. "I know, it's weird. And I understand if you're angry."

Though he didn't seem angry, not exactly. "Is it something you do on the side for kicks?" He picked up a snow globe from the desk and shook it, then stared at the white flakes drifting over a plastic palm tree as if what I said didn't matter one bit. Which was how I knew it did.

"I didn't do it for kicks. I did it..." How to explain? "I got roped into it by my roommate. I've never done anything like that before. I'm not a call girl. That's why I didn't respond when you emailed. That's why I couldn't see you again."

"Because you didn't want to admit you'd lied? Or because you couldn't have me as a repeat client because you didn't want to see me again?"

Oh God. "Neither. Both, I mean." I couldn't look at him.

He set the globe down. "I thought about you constantly. Every time I spoke to Persephone, or even her lawyer, God help me. Every time I sat on my couch. Every time I sliced into an apple. I still do."

He took a step toward me. I couldn't move. Didn't want to move.

"Are you saying you forgot me after that night? Are you saying you didn't feel it too?"

I was wildly turned on. Aware of his heavy breathing, his dilated pupils. His smell. His nearness. My own heart beating wildly out of control. My groin throbbing like he was going to take me against the wall, and oh, I wanted it. Desperately. "I didn't. I don't." My breathing gave me away. But if I told him the truth, I'd be giving him too much power over me.

He knew, though. He brushed my lips with his finger, the lightest touch imaginable, and yet it was the most sensual contact I'd ever experienced. "If I kissed you, if I fucked you right now, would you still feel nothing?"

"Try me." It came out in a near whisper. As if I was telling him a secret. And maybe I was, at that.

We stared at each other for a long, suspended moment, and then I grabbed him by the shoulders, or he grasped my waist, or we both moved at the same time, and then, thank God, then we were kissing. Lips smashed together, mouths open, bodies crushed against each other. Nothing gentle about this kiss, nothing tender. I wrapped my arms around his neck and brought him closer, sought his tongue with mine, and wriggled my body as close as possible to his.

This. Him. Right now.

I fumbled at the fastening of his pants. He inhaled sharply against my mouth. Apparently he hadn't thought I'd go through with it. But I wanted this so badly, I was shaking. Six long months living on the memory of one night. It wasn't enough.

Thankfully, Dylan took over, unbuttoning the

pants. I shoved them down his legs, exposing his impressive erection under a thin fabric covering. Thank God for the slit in his boxers. With a twist of my fingers, his cock was free. I slid my hand down the shaft, and he groaned.

"I can't—we shouldn't—this is crazy." His voice cracked, a broken whisper.

I put my fingers over his lips. "Crazy. Yes."

He grabbed my hand, sucking one finger into his mouth while his other hand reached down to my panties. I helped him pull them down. They dropped to the floor. Marie's carpeted floor. The office.

We *really* shouldn't be doing this.

I didn't care.

Dylan sucked rhythmically on my finger. The sensation was unbearably erotic. And I wasn't wearing panties. And his cock was hard and hot against my belly, through my skirt. He gripped my ass with his large hands, lifted me up, and slid inside. I opened my eyes, gasping at the sensation, only to see him staring at me, fierce and hungry, and that made me even more turned on.

"Do you want me?" His voice was husky.

"So much."

"Then why?" He shoved into me again, and I rode the rhythm, the building pleasure, my insides clenching around him. "Why didn't you want to see me again?"

"I did." I gasped again as he moved again, hard. Fierce. "I thought about you every day. Wanted to feel you like this." It felt so painfully good. Shivers up and down my arms, shivers inside my belly. "Inside me like this. Fucking me so hard." I inhaled. He watched me, intent, hungry. "So good."

"Have you been with anyone else since?"

"No. Didn't want anyone else." I tangled my hands in his hair. "More. Please. More."

He gave me more, and I nearly lost my mind.

I bucked up against him, rode him, my buttocks slapping the wall as I slid against him. I could feel his muscles straining under my weight as he held me up and pushed into me again and again. The feelings spiraled so fast, so intense, and, like a thunderclap that shook my body, I came. He pulled out and let me back down to the floor, and I gave a sobbing, shuddering breath. Even though I was done, the spasms receding gradually, making me weak and boneless, I didn't want to lose this connection, this link, this delicious, terrible encounter.

He staggered to his knees, clutching his cock. No condom. Right. I hadn't even given it a thought, caught up in that primal drive to have him.

I knelt in front of him and wrapped my hand around his erection. That was all it took. He came with a groan. I found a box of tissues on Marie's desk to clean up, then we collapsed on the floor, breathing into each other. Recovering. His pants were mussed, my skirt was a mass of wrinkles, and my panties were under my foot.

"Should I ask what I owe you?" Dylan's mouth had a sardonic twist that I didn't like.

I pulled away from him. "Are you kidding me?"

His gaze challenged, almost playful. "Shouldn't I?"

"God, no." I laughed, but it came out as more of a sob. "Maybe I should pay you. You're pretty talented."

"Good to know. So?"

"So?"

"What now?"

I stood, straightening my skirt as best I could. "Nothing. It happened. We got it out of our systems. We're done."

He stood too, picking up my panties from the floor. "Why are we done?"

Panic rose in my throat. He wanted to see me again? "Because you're getting over a spectacularly bad marriage, and I'm hardly relationship material. It was an amazing encounter. Can we leave it at that? If we go further, we'll screw this memory up. I'd rather keep it, thanks."

"What are you so scared of, Saffron?" His eyes glinted. He was using the wrong name on purpose.

"I'm not scared. It's not a good idea, that's all." I brushed my hair back into some semblance of a no-I-didn't-just-have-sex-in-Marie's-office coif and set my hand on the doorknob. "I need to get back to work. And don't you have a meeting?"

"Aren't you forgetting something?"

I frowned. "Can't we leave it at this?"

His mouth twitched as he proffered my panties. "This. I meant this."

"Oh." I wasn't about to put them back on, not after I'd stepped on them. "Throw them away." I patted my skirt. "No pockets."

He slipped them into his jacket pocket. That worked too.

I unlocked the door. Before I swung it open, he stopped me. "If anything comes of this…"

"A baby, you mean? Or an STD? Or AIDS?"

"I haven't been with anyone but you in a year. I'm clean. I meant a baby."

"Unlikely." He hadn't come inside me, after all.

"If it does, you know where to find me."

I nodded. Fair enough.

As I walked back to my drafting table, I avoided looking at my coworkers. I'd have to deal with them in the break room. It was all too obvious what we'd been up to. I cursed Dylan in my head. I'd kept my sexuality out of the workplace, and now he'd made it the first thing on everyone's mind. *Thanks a lot, pal.*

But that wasn't fair. What happened in that office was at least as much my doing as his. I had wanted it so much. Wanted him so much.

Could I really keep away from him?

Yes. I had to. If we started something, I knew in my gut it would get serious in a heartbeat. Hell, sex between a supposed prostitute and john—anonymous, no-strings-attached sex—had turned into an all-night confessional. What would a week, a month, a year of Dylan be like? My heart couldn't take that much emotional openness. A man like that—a strong, passionate man—he could tear my heart open with a spoon, leaving me hollow. Like my mother.

No. It was better this way. I'd figure out how to do uncomplicated one-night stands at some point. And maybe I'd eventually find a guy who didn't scare me. I'd move in with him, or he'd move in with me, or we'd get a house in the suburbs and commute into Manhattan and live a picture-perfect life.

Or maybe I'd collect cats and sleep under a big asexual fur pile every night.

But a man like Dylan, he was off-limits. He'd seemed to accept it at the end. He hadn't pushed again to see me. I wouldn't hear from him again.

I bent over my drafting table and focused on the columns I was sketching in. If they were square and spaced three feet apart, with wood beams along the ceiling in between…

My cell chimed, an incoming text. Dylan? My heart gave a traitorous leap. But no. Of course it wasn't him. He didn't have my phone number. It was Fernando.

Come into my office, I need to talk to you.

Was it against company policy to have mad sex with a potential client? Had I turned Dylan off to working with us? How bad was this going to be? Firing bad or reprimand bad?

Yearning for the dignity of my lost panties, I walked the long path between desks to Fernando's office. Naked and vulnerable was not a good combination. Even secretly naked. I felt off-kilter. Nothing about this afternoon was part of my carefully plotted out five-year plan. Dylan made me reckless. A perfect example of why I was right to avoid him.

Chapter Six

Fernando was facing away from the door, gazing out the window behind his desk. He slouched in his chair. His posture seemed irritable. Tense, at least.

"Sit." He spoke without turning around.

I sat. "Am I in trouble?"

He swiveled around. "Are you?"

"It won't happen again."

His eyebrows shot up. "What won't happen?"

"Whatever you think happened."

His eyebrows stayed up. "With Mr. Krause, I presume."

I glanced out the door, irrationally hoping for escape. No escape was forthcoming. Nothing for it, then. "I am deeply sorry if anything I did led to scuttling the contract. I know it's a big coup. I realize my behavior was unprofessional, but you have to admit it was also wildly out of character."

Oddly, Fernando looked more puzzled than angry. "He's not scuttling anything. He said he liked our preliminary work and thinks our vision is what his company is looking for. He needs to take it to his partners, but it sounds like they'll be on board."

Whew. "Glad to hear it. But...if you didn't know..."

"Know what?"

I rushed past that. "And he didn't decide to go elsewhere—then what did you want to see me about?"

The distraction worked. "You're on the Juniper project. As a second lead. It's a big commitment, a lot of late nights on top of your current workload, but you're on." He didn't look pleased. In fact, he seemed more like he was telling me I was relegated to the basement mopping floors.

I swallowed. It didn't help. I still felt like something large and uncomfortable was stuck in my throat. Second lead on the Juniper storefronts, presumably working directly with Dylan? I had a pretty good idea who came up with this gem of an idea, and his name wasn't Fernando.

Since I started at Alvarez and Associates two years ago, I'd been the best worker bee in their hive. I worked through lunch, stayed late finishing projects, and woke up in the middle of the night with remodeling ideas in my head. Got 3-D models and blueprints in ahead of schedule. Never spoke out of turn. Never did anything to ruffle anyone's feathers. I wanted this job to go well. I wanted a promotion based on my performance. I wanted to be Ms. Lilly, the outstanding employee, not Samantha the complicated human being.

And yet here I was. Exposed in every way.

Impromptu angry sex in the workplace, which apparently led straight to a promotion I hadn't earned, where my every move would be scrutinized and probably found wanting.

Damn Dylan.

No, I'd been equally complicit. Damn *me*.

That wasn't right either. The sex, yes, I'd been so caught up in the emotion of it—the rawness, the need—I'd forgotten myself.

But the Juniper gig, no. That was all his doing.

To my surprise, I said it aloud. "No."

"Excuse me?" Fernando leaned back in his expensive ergonomic office chair, his tone cool. But he looked less like he'd spit out a lemon rind.

I took a deep breath to steady myself. "I'm not ready for something this big. I'd be leapfrogging over half the office."

"Are you saying you're not good enough?"

"Not at all. I'm simply not ready. I will be, but not yet."

"Are you turning it down?"

"Can I?"

"I don't think that's a good idea."

"What if—" I realized my fingers were clutching the carved wooden arms of my chair so hard they were leaving tiny half-moon nail marks. I made myself relax. Breathe. Not think about Dylan.

So, of course, I blurted his name. "Dylan Krause."

Fernando rubbed his forehead as if he was warding off a headache. I knew the feeling. "What if Dylan Krause what?"

"What if he was okay with my withdrawing from the project? Would that be acceptable to you?"

Unexpectedly, he laughed. Of all the reactions I'd anticipated, this was most emphatically not one of them. "You have hidden depths, Samantha. I had no idea." He shook his head.

His phone rang. He answered it. "Alvarez. What's up?" As the person on the other end of the line started talking, Fernando hit Mute and turned back to me. "What is Krause to you? You didn't just meet him at a party, I take it." When I hesitated, he waved his hand. "Forget it. The less I know the better, I suspect. I agree, you aren't ready to take on the Juniper project. Do what you need to do to get out of it without burning the client. And good luck with your love life, but keep it out of the workplace in the future."

Before I could respond, he unmuted his phone and started talking to the caller.

I walked back to my table on legs that didn't support my weight very well, then sagged onto my stool.

Well, that was one way to make an impression on the boss.

I was going to kill Dylan.

Trouble was, I didn't know where to find him. The security guard at his office building sent me up when I said I was working with Alvarez and Associates, but the receptionist on the top floor gave me a puzzled frown. "Is he expecting you?"

"Fernando Alvarez sent me over to sort out some details after their meeting. I thought he called…?" I trailed off suggestively.

"Right. Of course. He does this. You'd think… Never mind." She paged through some documents on her computer. "He's at the warehouse. Come back tomorrow?"

Tomorrow felt like an eternity. My fingernails bit into my palms. I needed the release of yelling at the man right now, not some theoretical future date. Plus, I'd gotten out of work early today to go to a theoretical dentist's appointment. Unless I manufactured an emergency root canal and threw in a Vicodin stupor for good measure, I couldn't exactly sneak away two days in a row.

"Where's the warehouse?"

She gave me a skeptical look. "I don't think…"

I leaned in, lowering my voice. "It's kind of personal too. After that disaster with his wife, he and I…. And now he's…and I think I might…" I took a deep breath. "I need to talk to him. He'll thank you. I promise."

It did the trick. Her gaze softened. "He's been in a snit the past few months. Is that about you?"

I blanched. Because yeah, it probably was. My lie wasn't much of a lie, was it?

She gave me the address, which turned out to be at the Brooklyn Navy Yard, miles from the subway. As I walked from the F, the streetscape morphed from the familiar funky, intriguing area under the Manhattan Bridge to something more desolate and scary.

The Navy Yard was less exciting than I'd expected. All I saw was a large parking lot surrounded by long, low buildings. One had the familiar Juniper logo out front. Thank *God*.

The building wasn't locked, and there was no security at the front desk. No front desk, for that matter. Just a huge room filled with carved wood furniture. The place smelled of sawdust and wood oil.

Dylan was easy to spot. He stood in a clump with two other men and a woman, discussing a dining table. He gestured over it, his movement elegant and certain, but it was easy to see his unhappiness. The taller guy stepped back and talked a blue streak, wildly animated, obviously trying to convince Dylan he was wrong.

I laughed to myself. Convince Dylan Krause he

was wrong? Good luck with that. My guy had the worst case of the arrogant stubborns I'd ever met.

My guy? Where had that come from?

He was emphatically not, and never would be, my guy.

Now that I was here, I felt frozen in place. No way could I go over there and interrupt. It was impossible. Besides, why? I'd spent the past months running away from him. What was I doing running toward him?

I turned to go. I'd write him an email and tell him he'd crossed a line with his imperious demand that I should be included on his design team.

Why hadn't I thought to do that in the first place?

I made it to the door before a hand came down on my own, stopping me.

Dylan. I knew without turning around. He smelled like wood shavings with the faintest hint of musky sex. Of me. His body heat radiated, enveloping me.

"Saffron. How did you find me here?" His voice, low and controlled, rippled through me. "Looking for a repeat performance?"

"Don't flatter yourself." I swiveled toward him, hastily glancing around. His cohorts were safely out of earshot, down at the other end of the warehouse, arguing over an all-wood recliner that looked hideously expensive and even more uncomfortable, with knobs and angles where none should exist. I relaxed a hair. "I'm here to tell you I'm not working with you."

His eyes lit with a perversely amused gleam. "A phone call would have sufficed."

"I wanted to make sure you got the message. You can't tell my boss to put me on the account because you want to sleep with me again."

"What if that's not why I asked?" He still stood behind me, his hands braced on the door, but now that I'd turned, it was like I was standing in his embrace. Captive.

"Isn't it?" Was he going to kiss me? Would I let him if he did?

"Maybe I wanted to see you in action. In your real job." His tone caressed me.

"You can't. It doesn't work like that. I'm not ready. Linda and Blake would resent me like crazy. They've been at the firm years longer than me. And Fernando would be watching every move you and I made to make sure nothing inappropriate happened. It would be a disaster." The words came out in a flood, breathless and unsteady. "You can't march in and reorganize my life like you're my master and commander."

He let go, stepping back abruptly. "Why would I do that? I hardly know you, Samantha Saffron Lilly of the three first names. Maybe I wanted to make sure I saw you again."

I pulled my jacket tight, feeling the loss of his body heat. "Well, it was a mistake. Call Fernando, tell him you're fine without me."

"I will. If you go out to dinner with me."

Dinner. With this man. I must have licked my lips subconsciously, because I could feel a sudden coolness there, and Dylan's gaze sharpened, staring at my mouth.

But dinner led to drinks, which led to talking, which led to intimacy, both in bed and out. A date. A relationship?

My body felt both heated and chilled. Dylan's gaze challenged. And I had no answer.

"Friday night. Meet me at the Spotted Pig in the East Village. Seven o'clock. Then I'll let Fernando know we want to hire Alvarez but that you won't be part of the team. Deal?" The glint in his eye was more measuring than hungry.

It made it easier to say yes. It wasn't a date, after all. It was the next move in our bizarre game of chess.

On Friday at six p.m., I sat at my vanity, staring at my reflection. I'd outlined my eyes the way Jeanine had that first night, dark and mysterious.

I scooped up a bunch of hair and tried to pin it on

top of my head, but half of it fell out immediately, leaving my hair in semiplanned disarray. Now I looked like a ten-year-old tomboy with incongruous kohl eyes.

No, I looked like pictures of my mother from her last years. I glanced over at a framed photo I'd put on my dresser. She stared back at me, dark-eyed and painfully vulnerable.

I should get going.

I picked up the phone and dialed.

Three rings. Four. Five, and I was about to hang up.

"Hello? Who is this?" My grandfather sounded shaky. So frail.

"It's Samantha, Gramps."

"Is everything all right there? Do you need money?"

"Everything's fine. I've got a good job now, remember? I don't need anything." I picked up the photo and traced my mother's face with my finger, leaving a smudge on the glass. "I wanted to, I don't know, hear your voice. See how you were doing."

"I'm fine."

Someone murmured in the background. A woman.

"Do you have company? Should I call back?" I set the picture down.

"Oh, that's Hattie. My nurse. She's making dinner. Cabbage soup or something, I don't know. It smells like a swamp." He wheezed. "Is everything all right? Do you need money?"

My throat closed. His short-term memory had gotten worse. "I'm fine, Gramps. I have money. I have a good job now, remember? The architecture firm?"

"Oh. Right. Good, then."

I ran my hands through my hair, digging my fingers into my scalp. The barrette popped off. "How are you? Are you doing okay? Cabbage soup and all?"

"Oh, I'm, you know. Okay." I could almost hear his hand swishing in the air, gesturing to make the vague point. He cleared his throat. "Good you called. Good to talk to you. I'll talk to you later."

"Gramps, do you ever—" *Miss your daughter, my mother? Miss your wife? Miss me?*

But he'd hung up.

Chapter Seven

"Sam? Samantha?" Jeanine was at my bedroom door, silhouetted by the hallway light.

I closed my eyes again. "I'm asleep. Go away."

She flicked the overhead light on, blinding me, and came all the way into the room.

"Hey!" I put my hand up, shielding my eyes.

"What gives? She slid the photo frame out from my slack, sleepy grip. "That's your mom, right? Man, you're a mess."

"Did I say you could come in here and bother me?" I sat up, blinking hard against the light. "I'm pretty sure this is a violation of our roommate contract." I reached for the photo.

"She rises from the dead! Hallelujah!" Jeanine clutched the picture to her chest.

"Aren't you supposed to be out? With a client or something?"

"Early session today. He's got a date."

I rubbed my face, trying to wake up. "Wait. The guy's got a date, and he paid you to come over first and…"

"Give him a blowjob, yup. Stress relief. He really likes her. You should have seen him. He was so nervous. It was kind of cute. I hope things work out.

He hasn't had someone in his life for a long while."

Um, okay.

She narrowed her gaze. "Speaking of *dates*, what the hell, Sam? You agreed to a date and then stood him up?"

I glanced at the clock on my nightstand, though the darkness outside was enough of a clue. Nine p.m. I'd slept right through my date with Dylan. But… "How did you know about that?"

"Checked my email when I got home. Got a message with an all-caps subject header. Thought it was spam, but nope. Just one angry, sexy client."

"He's not your client." Dylan paying Jeanine to have sex with him? Dylan having sex with anyone who wasn't me? Jealousy lanced through me, spiky and unexpected.

"Maybe he should be. I'd treat him better." She eyed me. "You look like pigeons have been roosting in your hair and a preschooler drew your eyeliner on. Did something happen?"

"No. Yes." I grabbed a pillow, clutching it to my chest. "I called my grandfather. I was thinking about family, you know? And love. And…" I gestured toward the photo. "My mom. Love broke her heart. And she was his daughter, my grandfather's daughter, and I wanted to hear his voice. I don't know what I was thinking. It's not like he's going to suddenly be warm and cuddly."

Jeanine stroked the edge of the frame and handed it to me. "Before your dinner date? Isn't that a lot of baggage to haul to the restaurant with you?"

"Why do you think I'm home?" My mom looked painfully sad in the picture. She'd been maybe thirty-five. A year before she shot herself.

Jeanine tenderly smoothed my hair back from my face. "You really like him, don't you?"

I didn't look up at her. I couldn't. "Maybe. I don't know."

She stood, decisive, and grabbed the pillow away from me. "Problem is, you like him too much. You've put too much weight on it. Now it's about love and sex, all intensity and exclamation points." She gestured with the pillow. "No wonder you didn't show up at dinner. You'd lost your appetite. So you and I, we're going out tonight. We'll fix your face up and put you in a slinky dress and go to Krissie's engagement party at Greenpoint Pleasures."

"But I already told Krissie engagement parties weren't my thing."

"Then she'll be especially happy you showed up after all. And if you meet a nice guy, you're going to flirt and smile and not say no right away. Got it?"

It would be good to see our old coworkers, get a hug from Marina and Greta, the owners, and surround myself with music and laughter. But a guy? Not so much. After Dylan, they'd all seem like losers and wannabes anyway.

"Come here often?" The guy smiled at me, nearly a wink. Too bad. Before that lame line, I'd been admiring the way his cowlick gave him a certain boyish insouciance. But seriously? *Come here often?*

He laughed, showing his teeth. "Come on. Smile, at least a little. It was a joke. Postmodern, if you will. A parody of a pickup line. I mean, who wants to admit they come to a sex shop on a regular basis?"

"I worked here. For three years."

He slammed his palm to his forehead. "I put my foot in it, didn't I?"

I sipped my spiked punch, starting to enjoy myself. He was charming in a goofy sort of way. "I'm guessing you're a friend of Doug's. Any of Krissie's friends would know how much this place means to her. I'm also guessing this is your first time here. Sure, you've bought sex toys before, but online only and mostly just lingerie for your girlfriends, though you've eyeballed the cock rings and prostate stimulators and wondered if you dared."

His Adam's apple bobbed. "I'm that predictable?"

Definitely cute. "Go with the cock ring. It's fun for the whole family."

"You'd have to show me how it works." He gave me a wobbly smile. "That was an even worse pickup line than the last one, huh?"

I laughed. Behind him, Jeanine gave me a thumbs-up. I was tackling Flirting 101 with a modicum of success, for a change.

Beyond her, in the chattering melee, I saw a tall man standing by the lingerie, a plastic cup in his hand.

Dark hair. Handsomer than he had any right to be. Excruciatingly familiar.

What was he doing here, of all places? I'd stood him up for dinner tonight. Shouldn't he be home, throwing darts at my effigy?

"So what's your name?"

I swiveled back to the guy standing next to me. "Uh, what?"

"Your name. You do have one. Or do you all go by code names here? Like, you're Blue Lady." He indicated my dress, which was a shimmery indigo. It was also tight fitting, per Jeanine's specifications. With cleavage. Which he was staring into.

I glanced past his shoulder again. Dylan wasn't even looking my way. Did he know I was here? What bizarre coincidence had brought him to this party tonight?

He was chatting with Marina. Saying something amusing, obviously. She threw her head back, laughing, her glorious blonde mane shifting and settling like in a shampoo commercial. He grinned at her, revealing a dimple in his cheek I couldn't see from this distance but could picture perfectly.

Marina was married to Greta. He wasn't going home with Marina unless the two women had an open relationship, which was entirely possible. A couple who owned a sex shop together might well have decided to enjoy sexual pleasure outside their marriage. And Marina had an eye for an attractive man.

As I watched, she put her hand on Dylan's sleeve and cocked her head to look up at him. Definitely flirting. My stomach clenched.

"So what do you say, Blue Lady?" My would-be date looked at me expectantly. "Want to go somewhere quieter?"

I set my paper cup down on the glass counter, right above a display of pink and purple dildos in varying sizes, all exquisitely detailed to look like real penises. "Not interested. Sorry. You're nice and all, and you've got a cute embarrassed foot-in-mouth thing going for you. But I'm not available." To anyone. Which was why I'd stayed home. And why I should leave the party now. Jeanine could walk the fifteen blocks back to our apartment on her own.

And yet I shouldered my way through the crowd anyway. Go figure.

"Samantha! What a lovely surprise!" Marina enfolded me in a cinnamon-scented hug, her voluminous scarves enveloping me like a perfumed veil, then stepped back. "You should come by more often. We miss you. Any time you want to grab a work slot for old time's sake, let me know. Nobody knows this place like you do."

I glanced at Dylan, who was scarily impassive.

"Uh, hi."

Marina put her hand on his arm again. "This is Dylan Krause."

His eyes were dark. So dark. I'd had sex with this man. Hot, wild sex up against a wall. A few days ago. And I realized that I wanted to sleep with him again. Badly. I should have gone to dinner. Or skipped the meal and dragged him back to my apartment, cavewoman style.

I flushed. My whole body felt hot. He narrowed his gaze. Looked at my cleavage. Pointedly. It felt like a rebuke. I jutted my chest out so he could see it better.

Oblivious, Marina went on, "He's thinking about investing in the shop. Isn't that awesome? He's got some great ideas for a remodel."

Remodel? I loved the deep red sponge-painted walls, the neat metal shelving, and, most of all, the huge posters of buxom pinups from the '50s superimposed with incongruous slogans like *Embrace*

Your Inner Goddess, She Wants to Get Laid Too, and *Stilettos are My Superpower.* This place was my offbeat, off-kilter home, and I didn't want a single poster removed, not a single pastie, not one dildo. I wanted it preserved like this forever.

My dismay must have shown on my face, because Marina gave me a reassuring squeeze. "It's just talk so far. We won't do anything. Not for a while."

"At least you care about something." Dylan's emphasis on the word *something* was so slight, Marina didn't catch it.

She gave me a squeeze. "All our girls fall in love with the store. We take in the wounded and the lonely and make them family."

His eyebrows went up, but he said nothing.

"I wasn't as wounded as all that." I stepped away from Marina, giving her a smile to lessen the sting, then I turned to give Dylan as genuine a smile as I could muster, which was to say not much of one. "It's a great shop. I'm sure you'll do something gorgeous with it. Don't mind me and my quirks." *Seriously, don't.*

"Quirks?" He folded his arms. Game on.

"I'm not good at letting go. I'm also not good at holding on. Or doing what people tell me to do."

Marina's sly smile lit up her eyes. "You know each other."

"I wouldn't say that." Dylan's voice was ultradry.

Like scotch, it seared on the way down. "I would, rather, say I don't know someone at all when she stands up a guy for dinner without even calling."

"I don't have your number!"

"Your roommate does."

"Dinner? As in a *date*? Oh, Sam." She smacked me. "You don't stand up a guy like this. Not ever. You hear me?"

"Yeah. Uh. Sorry about that. I took a nap after work, and I, uh, overslept." I gave him a sideways glance. Which was a mistake. His face was alight with the same intense hunger I remembered from our night-long tryst, but with a hard edge.

"So reschedule." Marina spread her hands as if to say *problem solved*.

But rescheduling meant actually going through with it. I'd have to put on makeup, get dressed up for him, and leave the apartment with full, specific intent to go on a date with this potent, intense man who didn't let me get away with anything. Then I'd sit across from him at dinner in a quiet, upscale restaurant and make small talk. Be his date for the evening. It felt improbable. No, impossible.

Maybe that was why I'd called my grandfather. To make myself so miserable I'd have an excuse to stand Dylan up.

He spoke before I could. "No. Not dinner."

"No?" Now I was pissed. "Why not? Changed your mind? You don't want me?"

"I don't think we should do it. Not that way." His eyes glittered. He glanced at Marina.

She waved at him. "Go on. Nothing I haven't heard."

The music shifted, a song with a strong backbeat. Around us, people were coupling up to dance. Linda, who'd worked here the same time I did, grabbed a feather boa off the mannequin and wrapped it around herself as if she were doing a striptease.

I found myself leaning forward. "What way?"

"Same as the first time."

Sexual awareness flooded my veins. He wanted me. We could do it again. No strings attached. No relationship. Just sex. With Dylan.

"But in reverse."

I blinked.

Marina cocked her head. "Are we talking position, or..."

I grabbed Dylan's arm and pulled him away, leaving Marina behind. We were going to talk. In private. Now. Thankfully, he came willingly.

When we got outside, I let go of him. The street was busy, with people spilling out of the restaurant next door and smoking in the freight entrance doorway across the street. But it was more private than inside, and the music was muffled by the glass walls.

"Let me get this straight. You want to be my gigolo for a night."

"I prefer the term escort." His eyes gleamed with amusement. "It sounds classier, don't you think?"

"Is this some way of turning the tables on me? I stood you up, so now you're going to get revenge by— by what?" What would he do? Tie me up and leave me in a hotel room? It didn't make sense.

No, this wasn't revenge. This was something else. But he was clearly tense. His smile was tight and his eyes still glowed with that sharp, hungry look. "I want to make sure you show up. And if you're paying, you will, won't you?"

I nodded. My lips felt chapped. I flicked my tongue out to moisten them. He watched. My throat was dry. I swallowed. He watched that too. The air out here was cool, presaging winter, but I felt stiflingly hot. My cheeks, my chest, my groin. Throbbingly hot. This man. In my bed. At my bidding. All night long. Tonight? "So what now? Do we go to your place?"

He touched my hair, tucking a stray lock back into place. Oddly gentle. "Not tonight. I'll let you know when. And where." He kissed my nose—my *nose*—and then went off down the street, strolling past the late-night diehards on the restaurant patio huddled under heat lamps while they ate their fries. I could hear him whistling.

I shivered in my thin dress. My jacket was still on the pile of outerwear in the stockroom. I went back inside.

"I'll let you know when. And where."

Boyish Cowlick guy was chatting with Annie near the door. Good luck, dude. Annie wore her shawl like a shield and her lovely white-blonde hair pulled back. He was ignoring the keep-away signs, but he'd run up against them soon enough. She was seriously into her unavailable, unattainable boss. Awkward Dude didn't stand a chance. Too bad. He was rather charming in his way.

I nodded to them and squeezed past to get my jacket. On my way to the stockroom, Jeanine snagged me. "What happened back there?" she hissed at me. "He left without you."

"You noticed."

Wait a second. She hadn't asked who he was. Hadn't asked why he was here. And he'd said, *"Your roommate has my number."* She'd called him. Tonight. "You set me up. Again." I wrenched my arm away and stomped into the stockroom.

Dylan had known I'd be here. He'd planned this out. That explained the coolness, the calculating gleam in his eye.

Jeanine came into the stockroom behind me. "You

bailed on dinner with him. I thought you needed a nudge."

"You thought you should stage-manage my life. Again."

"Someone has to! You're not exactly doing a stellar job of it."

"Maybe I don't need a man in my life, have you thought of that? You don't have one. Not everyone needs a relationship, or even a hookup. I was perfectly happy with my vibrator until you set me up with Dylan."

"And since then? Not so much, right? You've been moping for six months straight. I live with you. It's been hell. Plus, there's never any ice cream left after your self-loathing binges. Being with him reminded you that you prefer boys to your plastic toy, but you're too scared of real emotions to act on it."

I grabbed my jacket. "Stop meddling. Just stop."

"Whatever. I was only trying to help."

"I don't need your help. I don't need anyone's help." I slid my arms into the sleeves. In my haste, I got it fouled up. My right arm got stuck, and the jacket was twisted around and upside down.

Jeanine grabbed the jacket from me, turned it right-side up. I took it back. "Thanks." Hard to thank someone when you're mad. It inevitably comes out like a scold. "I could have fixed that."

"I know."

I put my arms into the sleeves the right way this time. "I think I should find my own place to live."

"You do that. And remind me to never do *you* a favor. Fix you up with a hot guy? Forget it. I'm the devil. You screw things up with the hot guy? Heaven forbid I try to help you figure it out by, oh, *I don't know*, putting you together in the same room so you can talk like normal people do. Clearly I'm a bad friend. Got it. You can mess up your own life from now on. I'm done."

She flounced out of the room, destroying my own chance to make a huffy exit. I sank into the armchair, onto a pile of jackets, which puffed up around me, then subsided.

Jeanine. My best friend. I'd run into her in the college quad after my second attempt at a relationship dissolved in a pile of recriminations and miscommunication. She'd taken me to her dorm room, plied me with hot chocolate liberally dosed with schnapps, and told me firmly that I wasn't broken. She'd said nobody gets it right the first or even the second time, and that was okay. I knew she was wrong and that I wasn't built for intimacy—that I *was* broken, at least in that way—but I let her think I agreed. I loved having someone so confident on my side. The next week, she'd brought me here. To

Greenpoint Pleasures. Where I'd found a home with the other off-kilter souls in search of a nonjudgmental home away from home.

I owed Jeanine everything. I owed her whatever emotional stability I had.

I looked for her as I left the stockroom. We had to talk this out. We couldn't leave it alone, or it would fester and decay. I couldn't move out. I couldn't lose her friendship.

But when I found her, she was wrapped in the arms of a skinny, bearded redhead, kissing him like he was whiskey and she was on a bender.

I went home.

Chapter Eight

By the time Jeanine came home, it was dawn. I woke briefly to hear her giggling in the living room with the redheaded guy as they stumbled inside, shushing each other, and tiptoed loudly to her bedroom right across the tiny hallway from mine.

I put the pillow over my head to block out light and sound and the male intruder in my home, and went back to sleep. I'd have to catch her later.

But later came and our male intruder was still there. As I made myself a sandwich in our narrow galley kitchen, Jeanine didn't budge from her cozy perch on the couch, her legs thrown over the guy's legs. They had their heads bent over his iPad, watching something that was apparently hysterically funny.

"Do you want lunch? There's cold cuts but not enough cheese." I knew I sounded surly. I couldn't help it.

"Nah, we'll go down to the deli later." She lifted her head from the guy's shoulder. "This is Sean."

Sean nodded at me. "Pleasure to meet you."

"Yeah." It sounded so halfhearted, I belatedly blurted, "You too." Which made it worse. It just underlined the faux pas.

Did this Sean know what Jeanine did for a living?

Did he care? It usually made guys uncomfortable. On the other hand, he met her at a party at Greenpoint Pleasures, so maybe it didn't matter.

Jeanine gave me a sideways look. I wasn't forgiven for last night.

I should be the one forgiving her. I slapped together the two slices of bread, ignoring the mayo oozing out the sides, and sliced it down the middle. No, that wasn't fair. She'd meddled, but for the right reasons. Maybe.

Dylan.

Our arrangement.

I came halfway into the living room. "Have you checked your email yet today?"

"I did, not that it's your business." She went back to the iPad. "I want to see that again." She tapped the screen, and a loud noise bleated from the device.

I leaned against the kitchen counter and bit into the sandwich. Too much mayo. "Did Dylan email you?"

She frowned at me. "Should he have?"

Yes. He's supposed to seduce me. He needs to set a time and place for an encounter. But I can't tell you any of that, because you're not alone. And maybe you don't care anymore. And I miss you. "Let me know if he does, okay?" I took my sandwich into my bedroom and turned on the computer. I should get some work done.

And yet somehow I found myself doing a web search for Dylan Krause, Juniper Designs. I pulled up his executive profile, the one I'd seen that first day.

Chiseled jaw. Dark slashes of eyebrows. That hungry gaze, which seemed more like yearning to me now and less like pure sex.

Dylan. My boy-toy to-be.

Ha. That was a joke, a man like that acting the role of escort.

But he was going to follow through on it.

Wasn't he?

The on-screen walk-through glared from the screen reproachfully. My part of it was due to the group by the end of the day, and yet instead of working on it, I was on the phone, listening to it ring on the other end, then a click. I tensed, ready to talk.

Jeanine's cheery recorded message told me to *leave a message, yo.*

"Hey, you. You were busy with Redheaded Boy all weekend, and I'm happy for you and all, but we need to talk. Let me know when. I, uh—" I paused to formulate the thought. It seemed tacky to apologize in voice mail, but I had to say something. Before I could figure out the right phrasing—assuming there *was* one —I spotted a group of suits walking into the main room with Fernando. Five of them. One was Dylan.

"Let me know." I hung up.

Dylan's shoulders seemed larger in his dark blue tailored suit. He looked so formal, so professional. Maybe I'd ask him to wear the jacket on our rendezvous. The jacket and nothing else.

"What's that wicked smile about?" Rudy peered over the top edge of my widescreen monitor, holding a mug, a tendril of steam rising from the dark liquid. Coffee run, clearly. "Thinking wicked thoughts? You? Ms. I Don't Date?"

"Just because I don't date doesn't mean I have no interest in sex."

Wrong thing to say. His eyebrows shot up, and his smile showed a perfect row of white teeth. "Good to know."

Dylan walked past. He glanced over at us. I flushed and gave him a look that I hoped conveyed *it's not what it appears* and *I still want you* and *when do we do this thing?*

His mouth twitched, but he said nothing, not even hello. He just went past. As he walked down the row of drafting tables toward Fernando's office, I watched his ass in those well-fitted pants, grateful he wasn't one of those guys who stuffed a wallet in his back pocket.

Beside me, Rudy whistled quietly. "Those guys are something, huh?"

"What do you mean?"

"They stroll through here like they own us. It's kind of pissing me off. Especially since rumor has it we're going to have to work overtime on their stupid project."

"I'm not scheduled to work on it." Even though I'd stood him up for dinner, Dylan hadn't threatened to back out of our deal. I figured our upcoming liaison made up for it—assuming that was still on.

"I bet you are. Why do you think we have to hand in the blueprints for the Newark building ahead of our original deadline? So we can be free for Juniper. Fernando's going to tell us at the meeting this afternoon. They must be forking over a lot of money."

I must have looked dismayed, because Rudy shook his head and grinned at me. "Hey, I'm only grouching because I can't afford their furniture. It'll be fine. It's a good company. A good gig."

"I know. It's just hard to switch gears."

"True that."

I shifted my attention to the screen and slid my finger on the trackpad, signaling the end of the conversation. Still, I glanced down the row toward the conference room. The door was open. I could see a glimpse of dark blue fabric. A leg, seated. Dylan's?

He was in there. In my workplace. Again. And now his company had hired mine. To work for him.

If Juniper had hired Alvarez, if I had to work on the project despite myself, then it was all kinds of wrong for me to order the client around in the bedroom. Tell him to strip for me, tell him to kneel in front of me, tell him to lick my…

My computer beeped at me, a CAD program warning. I'd done something against code. What? I stared at it for a good two minutes before I realized I'd created an entire floor plan with no bathrooms, no doors, no access points at all.

The meeting lasted an hour and forty-one minutes. Not that I was counting. When they were done, Fernando came out, clapped Dylan on the back, and chatted with him as they walked down the row of desks. I couldn't even meet Dylan's eye without Fernando catching me at it.

Our liaison was a nonstarter. Dylan had obviously reconsidered. Maybe he'd decided it would be too complicated, what with my firm working for his. He'd ignored me on the way to Fernando's office, and he looked like he was about to ignore me again on the way out.

The thought felt like a rock in my gut. I'd had my first real fight with my best friend over this, and now I couldn't even have him for a single, greedy night.

Not that I wanted him. Just his body. And that hungry gaze, trained on me. And those whispered words. And that sharp intelligence.

This was not good. I didn't do relationships. Maybe it was just as well we weren't in one, not even for one night.

Yeah, I could keep telling myself that and maybe I'd eventually believe it.

After Dylan and Fernando passed by and my heart stopped skipping unnecessary beats, I realized there was now a folded piece of paper on my blotter. No doubt Dylan's discreet way of calling our assignation off. I unfolded it ever so casually, as if it were a normal note from a coworker.

The note only had a few words, written in a slanted, strong script.

Keats Hotel. 8 p.m. Friday. Check in as Samantha Saffron. Bring checkbook. Corset optional.

My body woke up. My nerve endings were alive, sparking like a child's firecracker.

It was going to be a long week.

I picked up my cell phone to call Jeanine, but put it down. She wouldn't want to hear from me. But before I could set it back on the desk, it rang. Her ringtone. I grabbed it. "I'm so glad you called. I—"

"Found another place to live? Good, because I have rights over the place, you know. It's my aunt's rent control." She sounded grumpy.

"I know. And if we break up, I mean, if we decide

to live separately, I'll be the one to move out, I promise. But we should talk through it first. Not make any hasty decisions. I miss you, and I'm sorry I got angry. I know you had my best interests at heart."

"You only like me for my apartment."

"Well, duh."

We both laughed. An uneasy truce. I leaned against the wall, looking out at the potted plants and marbled wallpaper.

"So what did you call about?" She still sounded wary.

"Do you have a corset I could borrow Friday night?"

This time her laugh was loud and entirely genuine. "Sam! What have you gotten yourself into?"

By the time I got off the phone, we'd agreed to go clothing shopping in Midtown on my lunch break tomorrow, and my head was clear enough to go back to work, though my body buzzed like I'd stuck my finger in an electric socket.

Was it Friday yet?

Chapter Nine

My heels struck the cement with sharp, distinct strikes. Under my light jacket, I wore an ensemble that made me feel like a goddess. The leather zip-up top fit me perfectly, and the multicolored skirt floated around my ankles. My shoes were gold, a fitting touch. I'd left off the panties again.

I hoped Dylan liked the outfit.

The Keats was a boutique hotel in the far West Village, amid the warren of cobblestone side streets. I walked through the ironically old-fashioned lobby with its inlaid tile floor and swirling cherub ceiling, and stopped by the gleaming mahogany check-in desk.

"I have a reservation. Samantha Saffron." A mellifluous mouthful. Did it sound as fake to her as it did to me?

She handed me a card key. "Room 302. Your husband checked in already, Ms. Saffron."

My hand spasmed, clenching the card key. *Husband.* This wasn't marriage or anything remotely close. This was an assignation.

There were no mirrors in this elevator, just dark wood paneling. It was like a tiny but perfect room. The doors opened to reveal the third floor before I was quite ready.

I paused before the door to room 302. Dylan was on the other side, waiting for me. Would he be in his bathrobe like last time? Wearing tight leather pants and a wifebeater? What was the male equivalent of a corset?

I fit the card key into the lock. The light blinked green, and I opened the door.

Dylan stood by the window, a slim fluted champagne glass in his hand. He turned from the view when he heard me at the door. He gave me a cool smile. "You're on time. Excellent. I prefer a punctual client." He was wearing a charcoal gray suit. Like the blue one he'd worn on Monday, it looked like it had been specifically tailored for his broad shoulders and tall frame.

I put my bag down by the door and stood uncertainly.

He gave me a slow, calculating smile, the kind that showed off his dimple but didn't light up his face, and proffered the bottle. "Champagne?"

"Sure." It might take the edge off.

He poured me a glass, then came over with it. Glided, more like. He had this *down*. "Take off your jacket."

After I shrugged it off, he tossed it onto a chair without looking. "Drink."

I took the glass from him, wrapping my fingers

around the cool stem, and took a sip. Champagne bubbles in my throat, tickling the roof of my mouth, dancing on my tongue. "Dylan…"

"Shh." He came around behind me and massaged my shoulders. "Don't talk. Don't think. That's what you're paying me for, Ms. Saffron. To think for you."

That name. So deliberate. All of this, so deliberate. Not a seduction, not exactly. Something else.

I closed my eyes and relaxed into the sensation. His thumbs kneaded my shoulders through the fabric. It hurt, and because it hurt, it felt good. I leaned back against him. "If I'm paying you, why are you still dressed?"

His hands stilled. "Do you want me to…?"

I turned, put my hand on his chest. *Mine.* The thought was fiercely possessive and absolutely terrifying.

"Not yet." I gulped down the champagne. "First I want you to take my clothes off." I touched the zipper nestled between my breasts.

His eyes got that feral look. "Whatever the client wants." He moved in, so close I could smell the sweet alcohol tang on his breath, and snagged the zipper pull. I braced myself, but he merely teased the pull, sliding it down a few teeth, then stopped. His fingers played along the top edge of the tight-fitting bodice, dipped underneath.

I closed my eyes, savoring the sensation.

"Open your eyes." A whispered command.

I opened them. "Who's the client here?"

"You need to stay focused. Get your money's worth." He leaned in and licked the edge of my ear. Sensation slicked through me, hot and urgent.

To hell with this. I turned my head and kissed him hard. He groaned, deep in his throat, but disengaged.

"First things first." He pulled my zipper down another inch, then kissed and licked down the exposed bare skin. Unzipped, licked, unzipped, licked, unzipped, and then he pulled my top off entirely, exposing my torso. He bent to take my nipple in his mouth, palming the other with his hand. It felt delicious.

It also felt entirely too controlled. Like Dylan was the professional he was pretending to be. Was he even enjoying this?

I tangled my fingers in his hair and gently tugged. He tilted his head, looking up at me questioningly. "Is my technique acceptable?"

I sat on the bed, my breasts tingling from the exposure to air. "I get it. You want to show me what it's like if it's just sex."

"I want to have sex with you, however that needs to happen. You're the one who doesn't want more." He sat on the bed beside me and stroked down my bare belly with one finger, then slid that finger beneath my skirt, skimmed the top edge of my pubis. I melted against his touch. A single finger. And he was still fully dressed. And it was sex and nothing more, no personal entanglements. The way I wanted it.

And yet... "When I came to your apartment in May, you asked me about myself. You wanted to know who I was before I—before we—"

His finger stilled. "I'd expected it to be a simple physical release. A way of exorcising Persephone screwing my best friend from my head. But when you walked in, all bravado and vulnerability, I had to know who you were and why you were there. What it meant to you. It turns out that sex *is* personal." He smiled, brief and wry. "At least, to me it is." He sounded more like himself now, and I was surprised how much that mattered to me.

"Does it have to be, though? Can't we just enjoy the way it feels?" I crossed my arms in front of my breasts, acutely aware of my seminudity.

Dylan laced his fingers through mine and pulled my arms back down to my sides. "We can pretend whatever you want. As long as it means we get to do this."

He leaned in and kissed me, his tongue seeking, probing, promising. His chin rubbing against mine, rough bristles against tender skin. I wanted to cry, and

I didn't know why.

When he broke away from the kiss, I murmured a protest, but he trailed a line of kisses down my neck, down my chest, and it was all good again. I sighed against him. But...

"I don't do relationships."

"I don't either. One bad marriage was enough." He sat back. My body missed him already.

"That doesn't mean I want to stop doing this."

"Good. Because we're not going to stop. Lie back." He indicated the bed.

I lay back. With his hands, he urged me to turn over, onto my stomach. I did. "But I don't need to know your favorite meal or your childhood pet or whether you're close to your parents."

His hands on my back felt slick with massage oil, his touch firm. Warming. "I'd have to go with sushi, but it depends on the restaurant. There's a place on the Upper East Side where you can only order omakase— chef's choice—and the chef decides based on your face what you'd like to eat that day. He reminds me of you. Full of rules and restrictions and very, very good at his job. I'd take you there, but that would be a date, wouldn't it?"

The thought felt almost okay. Almost imaginable. Sitting with Dylan at the sushi bar, joking and tossing down tiny cupfuls of hot sake. No doubt the bone-melting massage I was getting was messing with my head.

His voice got soft as he continued, like he was talking to himself, wrapped in memories. "For my fifth birthday, I got a gray cat named Oscar. He had a white splotch on his chin, like an old man's goatee. He used to pounce on my toes when I was in bed. He died while I was away at art school. I'd planned to get an off-campus apartment that spring so I could bring him back with me after winter break, but I never got a chance. He got hit by a car on our country road. And no, I'm not that close to my parents. They're good people, but we don't have much in common."

My breath hitched, and it wasn't only because of his skillful hands, now stroking down my back, soothing and arousing both in equal measure.

"So? Now that you know a few facts about me, do you want to go running out the door?" He sounded teasing but wary.

I looked over my shoulder so I could see his face. It was shadowed; the soft light from the bedside lamp flared behind him. "And Persephone? How did you meet her? Why did you decide to get married?"

Dylan's hands stilled. "I thought you wanted to have sex, no questions asked."

I sat up. "See? It crosses a line, right? It makes you uncomfortable. It's not just me."

He grabbed the champagne bottle from the nightstand and took a big swig. "We met in school. I was building a big wood frame for a sculpture project. I couldn't do it all on my own, so my roommate roped the entire ceramics class into helping. Persephone was this tiny thing. I thought she was going to collapse under the weight of the wood beam she was carrying. When I went to help her, she gave me a faraway smile and recited Auden. I was done for."

"You were a romantic." It fit. The hunger I'd felt in him, that constant yearning below the assured surface. Even the fact that he'd reached out to me after our night together. "You still are. You just don't want to be."

He leaned in and kissed me, tasting of champagne. Bubbles and bitterness. A fierce kiss. I felt it in my chest, in the back of my throat, in my gut. In high school, we used to call it a soul kiss, but it felt more like a soul-churning kiss. Intensely sexual but oh so scary. Still, I couldn't stop, *wouldn't* stop.

It was only a kiss, not full-on sex, no fancy moves. A kiss. How did it have any right to feel this good? I curled my fingers around the edges of his suit jacket and enjoyed the feel of the hard buttons of his shirt pressed up against my bare torso.

He groaned, deep in his throat. Groaned like he meant it.

"Samantha. I can't take much more."

"Good."

I slipped my hand beneath his shirt, heading south, dipping below his pants line.

He pulled my hand away. "I'm servicing you, remember? Not the other way around." He stood, shedding his suit jacket in a lithe, quick move, and tossed it on the chair in the corner of the room. Then he began to unbutton his shirt, revealing smooth skin with a light dusting of hair in the cleft between his pecs. When he glanced at me, I closed my mouth. I'd forgotten how beautiful the male body—this man's body—could be.

Dylan grinned, wicked. "You like that?" He slowed down his fingers. Unbuttoning one button and then the next, gradually revealing what lay underneath, smooth skin and rippled muscle. A businessman's striptease. The shirt sailed across the room to join the jacket. Now he was bare above the waist, like me. "Like what you see?" He cocked his hip, and for the first time, I saw the teenager he must have been. Serious, but with a mischievous streak.

Heat streaked through me. I got the sense that I was seeing a side of him he rarely showed people. This playfulness, this openness, it was only for me. My body thrummed with awareness, giddy and wild.

Dylan caught my gaze, and something changed in

his. The rest of his clothes got shed in a moment. No more striptease, no more silliness. He practically attacked me, pushing me back into the mattress. Kissing, fondling, his hands between us, my hands slipping down his bare back to his firm buttocks.

Dylan's phone rang. I stilled, expecting him to reach for it.

He ignored it entirely. Not even tightening in response. He was fully with me. And after a moment, the phone stopped ringing.

But we still had one barrier between us. My skirt. He yanked it down, nearly tearing it in his haste.

"Wait." I unzipped it and let it fall to the floor. Now we were both naked, skin to skin, heat to heat, his cock stiff against me. I opened my legs, slick and ready for him. Throbbing for him.

He pulled back.

I reached for him. "Now."

"I'm not done." He slid his hands between my legs, spread them wide, and knelt to kiss me there. "I want you to get what you paid for. All of it. Every single act, every single drop of pleasure." The promise in his voice was like a solemn vow. "I want you to enjoy this. Enjoy us, what we can do together."

"But it's not a relationship." It came out as a gasp as I levitated my hips against his mouth, an almost-involuntary reaction to the intimate pleasure of his tongue.

"Not a relationship. Sex."

"Sex." What he was doing felt so good. Like ice cream and ocean waves and all good things.

"With me."

"With you." I was melting, spiraling, tightening against his fingers, his mouth, his earnestness, his determination.

"Only with me." His voice stuttered, dark with passion.

"Always with you." And I came, a sudden sharp spasm of sensation and emotion, overwhelming and abrupt. I sighed into the diminishing contractions. "Always with you." It was a whisper.

Dylan nodded, almost grim in his intensity. He rolled on a condom, then sheathed himself inside me as I opened my body to him. All my nerve endings were still quivering from the aftermath of my orgasm. Taking him inside me was like a continuation, a prolonging of the pleasure, part of the receding waves of pleasure. I was hyperaware of his harsh breaths, the way his hair fell over his eyes, the way his legs rubbed against mine. I wrapped my hands around his hips, relishing the sharp strong movement as he grew sloppy and fast, gasping with the energy gathering in his body.

He pulled back. "But you—" Meaning: *you aren't ready to come again yet.*

"I'm good." Meaning: *I want you to come, I want to feel your pleasure.* Meaning: *do it.*

And he did. A few rotations of his hips and buttocks, then I felt him pulse inside of me, his whole body clenching. "Oh God. Samantha. Ohhh."

And he collapsed on top of me, nuzzling my ear. "Yes. Perfect." It was a whisper.

A whisper that sounded too much like warmth and coziness and comfort. I felt my body tense, losing the lazy boneless feeling too quickly. "It's just sex, right?"

"Just sex." Dylan sounded drowsy, almost drugged. He kissed my shoulder, then nipped it gently. "Just mind-blowing, awesome sex. What else would it be?"

Chapter Ten

When I got out of the luxe bathroom after freshening up, I expected to see Dylan where I'd left him, extravagantly sprawled across the bed, resting up for round two. Instead, he was struggling into his pants one-handed.

"When I said 'just sex,' I didn't mean you should leave after only—"

He turned toward me, giving me a shushing gesture, and I saw the phone held to his ear.

Deflated, I sat in the armchair, deliberately crushing his suit jacket under my bare bottom. If he was going to slip back into work mode, I'd leave a few telltale creases as a not so subtle reminder of our escapade.

Then I caught his words and forgot my pique.

"How badly was she hurt? Is she conscious?" He sat on the bed, his pants half-zipped. "I see. No, I understand. Yes, I'll come over now. I'm downtown, so it could take a while, depending on traffic." He looked around, clearly searching for a pen. I grabbed one off the spindly desk, and a pad of hotel stationary to go with it.

Dylan nodded his thanks and jotted down some information. A room number and a doctor's name.

"Okay, I'll be there when I can."

He clicked off and stood, properly fastening his pants. "I have to go. I'm sorry. Can we pick up next week where we left off? After all, you gave me the whole night, right?" His smile was lopsided and strained.

"What's going on? Someone's in the hospital?"

He hesitated. "It'll be fine." But it clearly wasn't.

"Dylan. What's going on?"

He snagged his shirt and shrugged into it. "Persephone was in a motorcycle accident." His face twitched, an involuntary wince, and I was thrown back. My grandfather's serious face. *I'm so sorry. Your father was rushed to the hospital last night. Your mom is there with him now.* He'd winced at my dismayed gasp. *"He'll be fine,"* he'd said reprovingly.

Dylan frowned at me now. "Are you okay?"

I rubbed my face. "Of course. Is she—do you know how bad it is?"

His mouth thinned. "Concussion. Fractures. A broken leg. She got lucky. She wasn't wearing a helmet. If she hadn't been thrown into the bushes..." He stared down at his shirt, which he'd buttoned wrong in his haste. "Crap." He started unbuttoning all those tiny buttons, fumbling with the holes.

I stepped forward, brushing his hands out of the way. "Let me."

He fidgeted under my ministrations. "I need to get going."

"Why did they call you? Aren't you officially divorced?"

"I'm still listed as her next of kin. Probably from the time she broke her arm two years ago. Her parents live in Minnesota, and her brother is in South Dakota." His body was taut, like a violin string strung too tight, ready to break. "Dammit. I shouldn't care. We've both moved on."

Tentatively, awkward as hell, I put my arms around him. It was the closest I'd come to a real hug in years. Decades. He hugged me back, so fierce I thought I'd lose my ability to breathe.

After a moment, he stepped away with a slightly embarrassed look and ran his hands through his hair to smooth it down. "I should get going. I'll let you know when we can pick this up again." He grabbed his jacket out of the closet.

I crossed my arms over my breasts, a feeble attempt to cover my nudity. *Good-bye* seemed inadequate. So did *I hope it goes well.*

I'm sorry might work better. Or even *I understand,* because I did, at least a little.

Instead, I said, "I'll come with you." And that, surprisingly, felt exactly right.

He paused, his arms halfway into his jacket

sleeves. "Why would you do that?"

I grabbed my top and shrugged it on. "Because nobody should go to the hospital solo. Because I'm here. Because I have nothing else planned for tonight."

Dylan slid his arms all the way into his sleeves and grabbed his bag. "Come on, then."

We made an odd couple, with Dylan all business in his charcoal gray suit and me all sexual suggestiveness in my leather bustier and diaphanous skirt. The clerk in the hospital lobby didn't seem to notice, but the nurse behind the counter gave me a sidelong look when Dylan announced himself as Persephone Krause's husband. I nearly told her I was the slutty mistress but stopped myself in time.

When we got to the room, it was empty. Not even a bed. And certainly no ex-wife.

"Maybe she's stepped out."

Dylan gave me a look.

"She's going to be okay. She's not in ICU or surgery, or the doctor would have said. She didn't tell you it was critical, right? It'll be okay."

I never went to the hospital after my father's heart attack. I was too young. But the image in my head was this: A sterile room, with monitors and tubes and mysterious machines. An empty room, no patient, the darkness outside like a tangible thing.

Beside me, Dylan huffed a sigh and grabbed me, kissing me so fiercely my chin felt bruised and my lips smashed. So fiercely I couldn't breathe. And even though it wasn't a remotely sexual kiss, I felt a flame lick up my insides. I was alive. He was alive. And here we were, kissing in a hospital room out of a creepy indie drama. It felt like it meant something.

"Dylan! What are you doing here? And who is she?"

We broke apart as a frail blonde waif of a woman was wheeled into the room on a gurney bed. She had a cast on one leg and a big, dark bruise on her cheek. As the orderlies positioned the bed properly in the room, she raised herself up on her elbows, wincing. Her wrists were painfully thin. It didn't look like they could support her. "Who are you?"

"Samantha Lilly. I work with your husband—I mean, ex-husband." I started to proffer my hand, then rethought it. She must hurt all over. "If you want me to go…"

She gave Dylan a reproachful look. "You didn't need to bring protection from me. I'm hardly going to attack you." She lay back down against the pillows as the orderlies straightened the pole and adjusted buttons around her, then withdrew. "What are you doing here, anyway?"

"I'm your next of kin on the form. The doctor

called me."

"You shouldn't have come. I'm fine." She coughed, which clearly hurt. "Dammit." She thumbed a switch that led to her IV drip, which presumably gave her a dose of some heavy-duty painkiller. "My throat is dry. All that poking and prodding and nobody offered me a drink. I missed lunch too. I went straight from the bike shop to the open road."

I poured water into a paper cup and handed it to her. She drank the water, then crumpled the cup in her fist.

Dylan frowned at her. "You bought the motorcycle today?"

She nodded. "A real beauty. You should have heard the engine purr. Like a big cat. A tiger or something."

"And you weren't wearing a helmet?"

"I ditched it." She grinned. "The feeling of the wind in my hair as I flew down the FDR was *amazing*. You should try it."

He closed his eyes. Whether summoning patience or emotionally wrought, it was hard to know. "You're lucky to be alive."

For the first time, something like reality seemed to creep into her awareness. "I know. The EMTs told me." She blinked hard. "But then, I've always been lucky, haven't I?" She gave him a wan smile. "I met you. That was my first lucky break. I didn't take good enough care of you. I took you for granted, messed around, and now you're gone. Like everything good in my life." She gestured for him to come over.

He glanced toward me as if asking for my understanding. I nodded. What else could I do? She needed him. He needed to be here for her.

Persephone hadn't even glanced at me. As if she knew I was no threat. Unexpectedly, the thought made my chest hurt.

When he got close enough, Persephone raised his hand to her lips. "My sweet Dylan, always looking out for me. You told me not to buy that motorcycle, didn't you? If we were still together, I'd still be whole."

"You are. Or you will be. It'll take time, that's all." He withdrew his hand, but gently. "You should ask your family to come stay with you for a while, until you heal."

"Family? I don't need them. I have Laurent. Laurent understands me. He says I'm a Pre-Raphaelite angel, that I was born in the wrong century. Can you call him? He should know. He should come be with me." She looked around. "Where's my phone? They brought my things into the room, didn't they?"

I cleared my throat. "Your phone might not have survived the accident."

She gave me an irritated look. "Who are you again?"

"Samantha."

"Are you Dylan's girlfriend? Or, no, his fuck buddy, right? The one who talked to me on the phone that time." Her voice grated, her tone such a contrast to her porcelain fragility, but the woman had been pummeled enough today. I clenched my fists against my sides and remained silent.

Dylan pulled away from her. "Samantha is a friend. Don't talk about her like that."

"Sorry." She gave me a glance under hooded eyes, clearly not sorry at all. She clung to his jacket. "I'm so glad you came. I missed you."

Seriously? Laurent one breath and Dylan the next? There was an easy solution, thankfully. "Give me your boyfriend's phone number. I'll call him for you."

And indeed, Persephone let go of Dylan's jacket. Her face brightened. "Yes. Laurent will come for me. He'll want to be here to help me through this. He'll change his mind. He didn't mean it. I know he didn't. My beautiful Laurent. He's a poet, did you know that? His words are so exquisite." She sounded dreamy. Drugged. The meds must be kicking in. "Yes, do that. He'll come for me and leave that crazy lady he's taken up with."

Which was how I ended up pacing past the nurse's station with my phone to my ear, explaining patiently to a man I'd never met that his ex-girlfriend—no, not

his ex? A short-term fling? Well, she didn't know that
—had gone on a mad motorcycle escapade and
crashed into a sidewall off the FDR Drive, and would
he come visit the hospital? "Yes, on the ninth floor. Tell
the desk it's room 914. Sure, bring flowers. That
sounds nice. No, she doesn't look terrible. Still pretty.
Yes, like sunshine and the promise of spring. Exactly
like."

I got off the phone feeling vaguely mournful. He'd
sounded baffled at first, like he hadn't known what role
he was supposed to play, but his light French accent
had become thicker by the end of the conversation, as
if in preparation for his hospital visit. Was anything in
Persephone's life real?

When I went back into the room, Dylan had
broken free of Persephone. She dozed in her nest of
tubes and monitors. The pulse-ox on her finger glowed
red. Dylan had his back to the door and seemed to be
staring moodily out at the 59th Street Bridge and the
Roosevelt Island tram half a mile south of us. The
night was illuminated by clouds catching and
reflecting the city lights. I wished I could see his face. I
wished I could touch him, comfort him. I wished—

I wished I didn't care.

I turned away. "I should go."

"Don't." Dylan turned toward me. "Please."

So I stayed with him looking out at the nearby skyscrapers and town houses and the low-rise warehouses across the river in Queens for what felt like forever. At one point, Dylan wrapped his arms around me and pulled me close. I stiffened briefly. This was sex, this wasn't anything like love; I shouldn't let him get the two confused, shouldn't let him blur the lines...

But I could feel his heart against my ear, his warmth against my chest, and smell his particular scent like warmth and goodness with an undertone of lust. And so I stayed. After a while, I even relaxed. I could allow myself this momentary indulgence.

Persephone woke up when her no-longer-ex-boyfriend walked into the room, as if she'd been faking sleep so she could become Sleeping Beauty awaking for her true-love-for-now. And Laurent, with his now-strong French accent, a hugely extravagant bouquet of deep red roses, and the cashmere scarf carelessly wrapped around his neck—he looked like the star of his own indie movie, with wind-chapped cheeks and sparkling gray eyes.

They embraced extravagantly, with many murmurings of "My darling, oh! I'm so terribly sorry," from him and "I missed you so!" from her. When he scooped her into his arms and kissed her far too thoroughly for a woman who'd just tumbled off a motorcycle, I nudged my shoulder against Dylan and gestured toward the door. We weren't needed. She'd moved on.

After we left the hospital, Dylan went looking for a liquor store. He found one two long blocks away. He bought a bottle of scotch. I could understand the impulse. As we exited onto the sidewalk, Dylan stepped into the street and waved down an oncoming cab. He opened the door, then paused.

I gave him a little nod meant as good-bye. "I guess this is it."

"Let me give you a ride."

"I live in Brooklyn." I pointed my thumb toward the bridge behind us. "I'll take the subway."

The cabbie peered out at us. "Are you planning to get into this taxicab or not?" Dark skin and turban aside, his querulous tone could have been my grandfather's.

I shoved my hands into my jacket pockets, feeling anything but sexy. "So. Been fun. Let's do it again."

Dylan ran his hand over the edge of the car door. "Let's."

And yet he didn't get into the cab. And I didn't seem able to motivate myself to walk away. I kept sending my legs the signal to move, but nothing doing. I'd have to stand here until he zoomed off.

Except that he wasn't zooming.

Oh hell. "I can come back to your place. For a little while. If you want."

Dylan bowed. "After you." A tiny, sad smile played around the corners of his mouth.

This was the right thing to do.

In the cab, he squeezed my knee but said nothing, just pulled the scotch out of the paper bag and took a swig. When he offered me the bottle, I shook my head. He drank in silence.

I gazed out the window at the dark silhouettes of trees flashing past the low wall dividing the road from the rest of Central Park. "Persephone is right."

"About what?"

"You're a good man, like she said. And one day you'll be over her. She'll be a distant memory that won't even hurt anymore, and you'll meet someone who deserves you. Someone as good as you are."

He laced his hand through mine. "I don't want someone like that."

A shiver ran through me, sparked by his touch. I stared resolutely out the window. "You will. You're not thinking straight right now."

As the cab emerged from the park and whisked us past the stately red stone fortress of the Museum of Natural History, Dylan let go of my hand and slid his fingers down my thigh, leaving a trail of goose bumps.

He leaned into me, whispering in my ear. "What if I'm not good? Did you think of that? What if Persephone was simply taking all the risks, creating all the drama for both of us?" His hand slipped under my skirt and crept up my bare leg. "I'm the one who booked an escort, after all."

"And acted as one tonight." It came out as a hiccuped breath. He was doing it to me again. His touch turned me on, as always, but there was something aggressive about it, something disconnected about the way his hands spread over my skin, blindly seeking, sliding his hands into intimate crevices. As if he wasn't touching *me*—rather, I was just a convenient warm body.

Walking through the fancy lobby this time was entirely different from the first time. The doorman nodded politely at us. Dylan wrapped his arm around me, tucking me close. Making me stutter in my stride.

This time, the mirrored elevator showed both of us. Showed him leaning into me, kissing me, unzipping my bodice.

I pushed him away. "What if someone gets on?"

"They won't. Nobody goes from floor to floor, only from the lobby up." He unzipped my bodice the rest of the way with a hard gleam in his gaze. "You make me feel reckless. You're my bad girl."

I pulled away. "I'm not."

"You're my hooker." His expression was wild, his eyes unfocused. "Mine."

"I'm *not.*" I yanked my bodice closed. This was getting weird. This was hands and grasping and all wrong.

He rubbed his face and stumbled back against the elevator wall, shaking his head at himself. "I shouldn't have said that. You're not available; you're not mine. You're not even really here." He sounded distracted.

The door opened on his floor. Someone stood waiting. An older man, pudgy and effeminate, with a tiny dog in his arms. He blinked at us as we got off the elevator, taking in my half-dressed state—my hands ineffectively clutching my bodice—and Dylan's off-kilter intensity.

"Miss, do you need my help?"

Dylan turned, and his neighbor's plucked eyebrows shot up. The next co-op meeting would be a doozy. "Mr. Krause. I didn't realize…"

"I think I'd better go." But he looked like a wreck. And even though he'd just pawed at me as if I was his own private sex toy, it felt odd to leave him like this. "Unless you want me to stay."

"No, go. Please go. I can do enough damage on my own." Dylan leaned against the elevator door to keep it from closing and fished in his pocket for his wallet.

"Don't."

"Money for the cab home."

"I'm in Greenpoint. I'll take the subway."

He smiled, grim. "I can afford the cab fare." He handed me a twenty. I shouldn't take it, but dammit, I wasn't ready to deal with the train, not like this. I took it. He took a backward step out of the elevator, looking like he was about to say something, but the door slid closed between us and that was that.

"Are you okay? If something happened…" The man's tone was kind, his eyes kinder.

I fumbled with my oversize buttons on my jacket, covering the half-open bustier as best I could. "Thanks, but he didn't do anything to me I didn't want. It's just been a rough night."

Dylan's neighbor nodded wisely. "Relationships can be tough." He grazed the top of his dog's head with his knuckles. "Worth it, though." The dog scrabbled in his arms, and he put it down on the floor. "She's a fussy one." He smiled at me. "Like me."

I smiled back, feeling a little better.

When the elevator got to the lobby, I waved good-bye to Dylan's neighbor and his petite dog, who was so eager to get outside she was straining at the lead, then I found a secluded corner by the elevator shaft. I opened my jacket, button by oversize button, then hooked my leather bustier's zipper and zipped it up. Shielded.

Secure. Ready to return to Brooklyn and down a pint of rum raisin ice cream with a chaser of regret.

Chapter Eleven

When I got home, I walked in on a poker party. So much for comfort food and mindless TV.

Jeanine was curled up on the couch under a colorful throw her mother had brought back from her last trip to Mumbai, peering intently at a fanned-out set of playing cards in her hand. A half-empty beer bottle rested by her elbow on the coffee table.

Our friend Annie sat on the floor, her knees up, her back propped against the bookcase. She held playing cards too, and nursed a mostly full bottle of beer. She wasn't so much studying the cards as gazing into them as if they could tell her fortune. From her expression, they had nothing good to report.

An unfamiliar dark-haired woman sat in my hand-me-down rocking chair. When I came into the living room, she set her cards facedown on her lap and smiled at me. "You must be Samantha. I'm Georgette. Jeanine and I are in the psych program at UCNY together. She speaks highly of you."

"Does she?" I quirked an eyebrow at Jeanine. "Good to hear."

Jeanine frowned. "What are you doing home? I didn't expect you back till morning. Did Dylan kick you out of bed, or did you only shell out for the quickie rate?"

"Ouch." I started across the room. It was the only way to get to my bedroom.

Annie gave me a wry smile as I went past her. "You had a bad date tonight too? Pull up a spot on the rug and help me feel like less of a loser."

"I don't want to intrude on your poker game."

"There's more cards." Georgette ran her finger along the top of the deck, riffling the cards. "Or you could join us on the next deal. We're celebrating my breakup."

I stopped at this. "Breakup?" She sounded so cheerful, she couldn't mean...

"I split up with my boyfriend tonight. By Skype, which was unfortunate, but he's in London and won't be back for a couple of weeks. I thought this way he'd have time to adjust to the idea. He didn't take it well, I'm afraid. He says I have to be out before he gets back."

"Maybe you can move in with me." Jeanine gave me a sideways glance. "I might have an opening."

"Jeanine is sadly mistaken. She and I are best friends and she thinks the world of me. I'm not moving out." I sat on the arm of the couch, right by her.

She gave my hand a quick reassuring pat before tossing a chip on the coffee table. "I raise fifty cents."

"Big spender." I grinned at her.

"Don't you know it."

Georgette put her cards down. "Too rich for my blood. I fold. I'm ready for pizza."

Annie frowned over her cards. "Wasn't your friend bringing it by?"

"Alanna? She's probably gone off on an unexpected adventure and forgotten about food. She'll remember eventually. You don't mind cold pizza, do you?" Georgette smiled gently, clearly amused at her friend's foibles.

As Annie dealt me in on the next hand, she told us about her date gone sour. She'd gone out with Goofy Cowlick boy from the Greenpoint Pleasures party, and he was charmingly stumble-footed and geeky, and she'd laughed and enjoyed herself, "And I didn't even think of-of anyone else, not even once. And then he kissed me, and it was… I don't know. *Nice*." She shook her head like she was relating a disaster. "Then he asked me if he could come in for a drink. And I froze."

"Not interested?"

"Not even a little." She set the cards down. "There was nothing wrong with him. Absolutely nothing. Which is exactly what I felt when he kissed me. Nothing. I'm never going to have sex again."

"Join the club." I stared at my miserable hand. "And I'm not even lucky at cards." I discarded as many as I could.

Jeanine sat up, her blanket drifting onto the floor. "Seriously? You and Dylan have so much chemistry, you broke the thermometer. I saw how he was looking at you at the party. Like you were on the menu."

Annie's eyebrows shot up. "He's *that* guy? I saw you two talking, and yeah. I agree. So what went wrong?"

"His ex-wife smashed up her motorcycle on the FDR, and she wasn't wearing a helmet. She's got a concussion and some broken bones. She's lucky she's not paralyzed for life, but she's gushing over Dylan one minute and flirting with her new guy the next, all while lying in a hospital bed looking like a bruised and battered fairy princess. It's enough to give anyone whiplash."

"And he's alone now?" My roommate shook her head at me. "Have I taught you nothing? The guy needs some comfort, not alone time."

"He didn't want comforting. He wanted mindless humping."

Annie gazed thoughtfully at me over her cards. "Isn't that what you're always saying you want? Sex and nothing more? Did you not mean it after all?"

Ouch. I had to sit down tonight with the two people who could see through me, didn't I?

Georgette picked up two cards from the pile.

"Love's complicated, isn't it?"

"It's not love. It's not. It's—the guy is—I like him. I thought we shared more than just…"

"Just sex?" Jeanine's eyes gleamed.

"I—uh." I stopped, started again. "I mean, okay, yeah, it's not just sex, but it's also not—" I snatched the new cards up, clutching them too tightly. "Isn't there something in between? Friends with benefits, maybe? Where it matters but it also doesn't have to mean anything big?"

All three of them were giving me skeptical looks now.

I grabbed Jeanine's beer bottle and took a deep swig.

"Hey!" She reached for it.

"Sorry." I handed it back. "Don't expect me to make sense. It's been a rough night. Dylan was… His ex has done a number on him, and seeing her in the hospital like that…"

"And you're not there because…" Jeanine rubbed her shirtsleeve across the top of the bottle, wiping it clean.

"Because things got weird. Like I said." That look in his eyes, voracious but not seeing me. Blind, almost.

"He visited his ex in the hospital and reacted strangely afterward? That's not exactly a big shocker."

Unsettled, I flicked my thumb through my new

cards. "He was getting drunk. In the cab." Which could account for some of his behavior, couldn't it? "Dammit. I overreacted. I should go back. He shouldn't be alone tonight."

Jeanine grinned at me. "Look at you, being all empathetic and stuff."

Georgette rearranged her cards. "Be careful. He'll be vulnerable." Her gaze was troubled. "You might find yourself in deeper than you anticipate."

"Says the woman who never ventures into the deep end of the pool. Who broke up with her boyfriend over Skype." Jeanine raised her eyebrows at Georgette.

"Ouch." Georgette grimaced. "Point taken."

Jeanine turned to me. "Don't listen to her, Sam. Go for it. Dylan needs you tonight. Think of it as your own personal brand of therapy." She winked at me.

I set my cards on the coffee table. "I'm folding."

"More like you're calling and raising the stakes." It turned out Georgette had a dimple when she smiled.

Annie took a swig of beer. "More power to you. I need to borrow some of that courage." She was obviously thinking about her professor crush.

"Isn't he married?"

"Widowed." She tossed two chips onto the table. "I'll see you and raise you. Whoever's still in the game."

The doorbell rang. I went to open it. A woman a few years older than me stood there, holding two pizza boxes. Her blond hair was falling out of her clip. She blew it off her face. "Anyone hungry?" She smiled at me in greeting. "Alanna Woodruff. I come bearing food."

"Samantha Lilly. I'm not here." The pizza smelled enticing, the company welcoming, but I had somewhere to be. "Talk about a man like your heart is breaking, and you'll fit right in."

She blew again on her bangs and exchanged glances with Georgette. Something passed between them. Some story there. "Sounds like loads of fun. Anyone have a sledgehammer we can knock ourselves on the heads with after we're done with that?"

I tried to glide through Dylan's lobby like I belonged there. I didn't entirely pull it off. The doorman called me back.

I gave him an airy wave. "Call up if you want, but he's expecting me. You remember me from earlier, right?"

"You know where you're going?"

"I do." And that was all it took.

When I got off the elevator on his floor, I strode to Dylan's end of the hallway and rang the bell without stopping to consider. Momentum, that was key.

"It's open. Come in." His deep voice was muffled by the thick door.

I swung the door open.

Dylan was seated at the dining table. He looked more disheveled than when I'd left. Hollowed out. He'd half-unbuttoned his shirt, and his feet were bare. A row of shot glasses lined the placemat in front of him, and he was carefully pouring a dollop of dark gold liquid into each. "Leave it by the door."

I stepped in and closed the door.

He looked over. "You're not sushi."

"Should I go get some?"

"I ordered it half an hour ago." He gulped down a shot. "Why are you here? You left. I was inappropriate or something." As soon as he set the glass down, he picked up another one, raising it to me in an ironic salute. "Here's to mixed messages." He gulped it down and grabbed a third. "And here's to complicated women." He drank that down.

I shouldn't have come. I gripped the still-open door for support. Standing in the doorway, neither in nor out. Undecided. Frozen.

Dylan stood, accidentally knocking over two of the empty glasses with a sweep of his arm. He didn't seem to notice. "Come on, then. Let's get to it." He headed toward the bedroom, pulling off his T-shirt as he went and tossing it toward the couch.

When I didn't follow, he paused. "What are you waiting for? It's what you came back for, isn't it?" His bare chest was side-lit by the light streaming from the kitchen, which picked out the strong curve of his pecs and the slope of his abdomen.

"I don't want to be your fuck buddy tonight." The door was reassuringly solid beneath my tight grip.

"Then what do you want?"

"To be your friend." I let go of the door. It swung back into place and latched with a resounding click.

"I don't have friends. Persephone took all our friends in the divorce. Along with the fish tank and the wedding silver." He went back to the dining table and the row of shot glasses.

"You have one now. A friend, I mean. Not a fish tank."

His mouth quirked. "Well, then, friend. Come help me get stinking drunk." He picked up a glass and held it out. The liquid glistened.

I came into the room, finally committing to being here. I took the shot glass from him, letting the cool curve rest against my palm.

He grabbed another and gulped it down, not even wincing at the burn, then picked up another, the last one in the row. "Not drinking? You're supposed to keep me company."

"I'm here. I'm keeping you company."

"Hmph." He drank down the last glass and picked up the bottle, uncapping it.

"Does it help? Does it make you numb?" I gazed at the slow swirl of liquid in my glass.

"No." He poured a measure of whiskey into a glass. "But it'll allow me to sleep tonight. Since you won't have sex with me, what else have I got?"

"If I gave you a blowjob, would you stop drinking?"

He set the bottle on the counter. "You offering?" His voice was thick, but not with desire. With alcohol and unshed tears.

"Are you still in love with her?" I gulped down the contents of the glass. It burned a hole through my esophagus but cleared my head. I saw everything with startling clarity. I cared about this man. Despite myself, I did. And his pain hurt me. How had that happened?

He got up, bringing the bottle with him as he went to the couch. Even now, so drunk he radiated ninety-proof vapor in a trail after him, he moved with grace and power.

I set my glass down on the counter and followed.

The doorbell rang. "That would be the sushi." He went to the door to get the delivery, giving me a much-needed breather.

I gazed around the large, beautiful but still

somehow unfinished space. He'd decorated the living room in the time since my last visit six months ago. Instead of packing boxes on the side of the room, there was a glass-topped side table with elegantly carved pale wood legs nestled next to the armchair I remembered from last time.

It was the most stunning original armchair I'd ever seen. It looked like it had organically grown from a single tree trunk, with a sense of the gnarls and beautiful imperfections of nature—and yet the curve of the seat was perfectly, ergonomically designed to mold to a human body for maximum comfort. The kind of chair you'd curl up in to reread your favorite novel or listen to your favorite torch singer.

Dylan came back with a shopping bag. He set takeout containers on the coffee table, which was another curved, polished slab of wood, clearly from the same designer. Him?

"You hungry? I got plenty." He sat on the couch.

"If it's okay." I selected a hand roll and nibbled cautiously. Raw fish made me squeamish. I usually ordered tempura. It was battered and fried and completely safe.

He watched, amused. "It won't bite. It's no longer alive."

"It's not cooked. It could still get lively." I chewed slowly, evaluating the unfamiliar texture of seaweed, slightly sweet rice, and smooth fish.

"So?"

"Not bad."

"It's not the place I told you about. Just a takeout joint around the corner."

I took another bite, this one more bold. "I might want to try that other place. Sometime." I avoided looking at him.

"I could take you."

"Or you could tell me the name."

"Friends take friends out to dinner all the time."

Now I looked at him. He gazed back, oversolemn.

Right. He was drunk. I'd forgotten.

We chewed in silence for a few minutes. Dylan seemed pensive and far away.

It was too much. "You never answered my question. Are you still in love with Persephone?"

He selected a tuna sushi log, the deep red fish a stark contrast to the whiteness of the rice, and popped it into his mouth whole. He took his time chewing.

"Forget I asked. None of my business." I took a piece of a sushi roll from the tray in front of me, wrapped it in a thin slice of ginger, and dipped it in a puddle of soy sauce.

He picked up another piece of sushi and smoothed a slice of ginger over it with his thumb. "We were so young. I didn't think so at the time, but we were babies. And she was so lovely. And her wild, random ideas, they seemed exotic and exciting. Even her neediness made me feel like I was important." He put the sushi down untasted and leaned back against the couch. "By the time it got truly bad, I was in too deep to make sense of it. She'd wail and tell me I was a terrible husband. That I was the reason she'd turned to other men. I wasn't loving enough, I was too caught up in my job, I was never there for her, I wasn't proof against the monsters in the dark." He trailed off briefly, lost in memories. "I bought into her version of our marriage. Even after I left her, on some level, I thought it was my fault."

I laced my fingers together, tight.

His eyes were dark with wide-open emotion. "And then tonight…"

"Tonight you realized it wasn't you."

"It was never me." He sat up, overbalanced, then self-corrected. "All that pain. All for nothing."

"She got into that motorcycle accident on purpose, didn't she? So she could get Laurent to pay attention to her."

His mouth twisted. "Maybe not entirely on purpose, but somewhere inside, she knew it was stupidly reckless. She had to know."

I knew what Jeanine would diagnose. "She's a classic borderline personality. She's nothing without a human mirror reflecting herself back at her."

"I fell for it. Ten years of my life, sucked up by a human vacuum, hungry for emotion." He held his head in his hands. "God, I need water."

I went to the kitchen. The faucet was old and rusted. It creaked as I turned it on, and water poured out in a rush. He'd furnished the place but hadn't upgraded anything. My architect self muttered annoyance in my head. Dylan had the money. Why not hire someone?

When I returned to the living room with a full glass of water, Dylan was stretched out on the couch, asleep.

Now what? I took a sip of water and contemplated him. His dark lashes, the strong line of his jaw, his sculpture-perfect cheeks—they were surface. They were what I'd seen in his posed portrait on that website for Juniper Designs. But up close I saw the subtle vertical lines between his eyebrows that suggested troubled thoughts and foretold what he'd look like in fifteen years. I saw too the way the skin on his bottom lip was rough and uneven, as if he'd worried it with his teeth. And the way his hair curled around his ears, hinting of hidden wildness, barely suppressed passion.

I smoothed his hair, which was soft and yielding under my touch. He didn't stir.

I ran my finger along his cheek, feeling the rough

stubble against my sensitive fingertip, then the contrasting softness of his lips. He moaned, almost inaudible. His eyes flickered but didn't open. Dreaming?

Hesitant, wondering at myself, I knelt and gently kissed him, trying not to wake him. Breathing into him.

I startled as Dylan's arms came around me, pulling me closer. My feather-light brush of lips turned into a genuine, two-way kiss. His eyes were still closed, and he murmured deep in his throat even as he sucked and nuzzled against my mouth. I was pretty sure he was half-asleep, but I felt the embrace in my chest, warm and alive, as my fingers tangled in his hair and pulled him closer.

It wasn't lust, not exactly. Sure, I could feel that too, a pulse in my groin, but this was something else. Something better. I could stay here forever like this. Held and holding. Comfort and contact and warmth.

Was this what my mother had felt when she was with my father, this sense of rightness and belonging? Was this why she'd killed herself after he died? Because she felt empty without it, without him?

I pulled away and scrambled up, away from Dylan's seductive whiskey breath and those insanely sweet lips. Pulling myself together, I grabbed my jacket and shoved my arms into the sleeves.

He raised himself up on his elbows. "You're going again?" He looked sleep smeared and well kissed. And far too lovable, dammit.

"Go back to sleep. Take two aspirin when you wake up. You're going to have a killer headache. Take care of yourself, okay?"

He lay back down, his eyes closing. "Yes, ma'am."

As I headed for the door, I heard his voice behind me, soft and sleepy. "Thank you for coming, Samantha."

Just before I clicked the door shut behind me, he added, "Friend."

Friend.

　Lover.

Words like rapid heartbeats as I strode down the lonely Greenpoint sidewalk on my way home.

　Entangled.

　Vulnerable.

Scary words. Dangerous words.

Maybe I should have gotten drunk after all.

When I stepped into my apartment, I found the remnants of the poker party. They'd eaten all the pizza and left the paper plates stacked on the coffee table. Annie was gone. Jeanine had gone off to bed. Georgette was stretched out on the sofa under my grandmother's afghan, lightly snoring.

Only Alanna was awake. She was sketching something on the back of a pizza box. "The game is over, as you can see. Your roommate cleaned us out. I should go."

"No, that's okay." I set my stuff down.

"It's just—my apartment is too quiet. My brother's up in Boston for an overnight, meeting with a prospective client. And I'm..." She shook her head. "I'm not good being alone with my thoughts right now. Everything echoes inside my head, and it makes it all worse. But I'll go." She looked as bleak as I felt.

When had I become the repository for everyone's pain? Me, the one who corralled my heart off with barbed-wire fence posts.

But I picked up the pizza box. Alanna had sketched Georgette, asleep on the couch. She'd captured the crease the edge of the throw pillow was making against Georgette's cheek, her friend's wide cheekbones, a stray curl falling across her forehead. "You're an artist."

"Yeah. I've worked at a few ad agencies. You've probably seen my stuff on TV. The toothpaste commercial, the one where you see the important moments in a girl's life?"

"Where she loses her first tooth and then the kiss with braces where they get stuck, and the hilarious wedding cake...?"

"That's the one." She sounded wistful.

I sensed a story, but it was late and I was tired. I gave her back the pizza box and went to the kitchen, where I grabbed a bottle of coconut water and uncapped it.

Alanna went back to sketching her friend's sleeping visage on the pizza box. "Your roommate told us about the fake call girl thing."

I spilled liquid on my top and quickly blotted it with a kitchen towel. "Did she also tell you it was her idea? That he was supposed to be her client?"

"So she actually *is* a call girl? For real?"

I screwed up my mouth, annoyed for no good reason. "For real. But it's not like you think."

"Whatever. We all have secret lives, right?" Her blond head bent over her work, but her foot came up to rub against her other calf. "It's none of my business, so tell me to shut up if you want—but don't let him think you're something you're not. It'll bite you in the ass."

"Don't I know it." I chugged the rest of the drink and tossed the bottle toward the bright blue recycling bucket. "He knows, though. He didn't, that first night. But he found out." *And that was when things got complicated.* I faked a yawn. "I'm off to bed. Stay as long as you want."

I went to my room and closed the door softly,

stripped out of my clothes, and slipped under the chilly sheets. But I could hear Alanna's pen softly scratching on the cardboard out in the living room, Jeanine's sleep snorts from her bedroom across the hall, and the sounds of a city night out the window: a dog bark, a distant siren, a foghorn on the river. Light played on the ceiling, and my memories played in my head. Me with Dylan, my parents together. My mother alone. Persephone, looking mournfully at Dylan, knowing what she'd lost, and then so painfully false with her French lover. I didn't fall asleep until long after Alanna left the apartment, the door latch clicking quietly into place behind her.

Chapter Twelve

Monday morning, I was standing by the coffeemaker at work waiting for it to finish brewing when Fernando came by, dressed in a bright blue blazer and fiery red-orange tie. He looked like a Playmobil version of a corporate executive.

"Morning, Samantha. Glad you're here. I need you on Juniper."

"But I told you I didn't—"

He waved at me. "That was preferential treatment. That would have been wrong. This is me. I need your skill set. And it doesn't hurt that you know Krause, since you'll be reporting to him."

"But that would be—" I hesitated, then dove in. No secrets. "What if he and I—what if we'd had something?"

"Romantic, you mean?" He looked amused.

I could feel the heat in my cheeks like a bonfire. "Yeah."

"Are you currently seeing him?"

Friday night, sex in the hotel. Friday night later: *"Thank you for coming, Samantha. Friend."*

Maybe. "Not exactly."

"Did you end things amicably?"

"I guess."

"Then I don't see a conflict. But tell me if things get strange."

"And you'll take me off the project?"

"No, I need your analytical eye. You can report to someone else at Juniper, if need be. I'll talk to him about it today, make sure things are squared away. Just in case."

The coffee finished brewing with a burble and a pout. Fernando snagged the mug I'd chosen and poured himself a cup. I pictured the conversation between Fernando and Dylan: *Are you sleeping with her? What are your intentions?*

"You know what? It'll be fine." I gave him as sincere a smile as I could manage and took another mug down from the cabinet.

After I'd doctored my coffee with a big dollop of milk and two teaspoons of sugar, I emailed Dylan. *It looks like I'll be working under you. What do you need done?*

He emailed back right away. I winced at the sexual innuendo I'd left myself open to, but his email was equally straightforward. *We're considering a potential storefront property. Go to the location. Take photos of every angle, and measurements too. Email them to me ASAP so we can nail this down.* He included the address.

He hadn't signed it in any personal way. Just

his .sig.

I stared at the email for a long moment. Really? Nothing personal at all? Never mind that mine was strictly professional. I was the underling. I had to be excruciatingly correct. But Dylan could have said *thanks for Friday night.* Or *I had a bad hangover.* Anything.

Was he having second thoughts about how vulnerable he'd been Friday night? Was that it?

My stomach felt sour. I got up to check on the expiration date of the milk I'd used in my coffee. In retrospect, it hadn't tasted right.

The milk was good through the end of the week. It smelled sweet and creamy. I tilted my head back and let a drop fall onto my tongue. It tasted like butterfat childhood.

"Samantha! What are you doing?" Rudy was staring at me as I put the carton down.

"I didn't touch it to my lips. Don't tell anyone."

"Of course not." He still stared at me.

"Do I have a milk mustache?"

"You seem different." His gaze swept over my outfit, then back up to my face. "Unbuttoned."

I felt my blouse reflexively, realizing I'd left the top two buttons undone this morning. I was showing a hint of cleavage for a change. I almost fastened them but dropped my hand. After all, why not? Fernando hadn't objected. I was still work safe.

"No, you look great. Kinda hot." He raised one eyebrow. "Is that okay to say? Will you report me for sexual harassment?"

I smiled wider than I'd intended. "I can handle it."

He grinned back. "You're changing. I like it. If you want to reconsider hanging out with me outside of work, let me know. Offer's still open."

I could, at that. Test Rudy's kiss against Dylan's, see if my body responded to his light, playful touch. "I'll think about it."

His mouth twisted. "Never mind."

"No. Really. I will."

He nodded. "Good, then." He rummaged in the office fridge and pulled out a tray of cut-up cantaloupe, then went off to his desk to eat.

My flirtation with Rudy made it easier to go to the job site and not think about Dylan the entire time I was there. Just half the time. Maybe three quarters. But in my defense, it was on Seventy-Second Street between Amsterdam and Columbus, close to his apartment. I'd strutted past here in my high heels that first night, back in May. This storefront had been an indie bookstore. Empty shelves still lined the walls and empty magazine carousels adorned the center space, as if waiting for a new shipment.

All quiet now. Not unlike my life. My

circumscribed, self-limited life.

What had Alanna said? That silence made her thoughts echo unbearably?

I took shots from multiple angles, jotted down measurements, and got out of there. It wasn't a suitable space anyway. Not enough light. Too narrow. Fine for a bookstore, where you could get lost in the stacks, but not good for a furniture store where the pieces had to glow with invitation and the promise of a good life.

It was starting to drizzle as I walked to the subway. I hesitated before crossing Columbus. Dylan's apartment was one block north. He wouldn't be there, of course. He'd be at work.

I walked to Central Park West in the rain and took the subway downtown. I didn't get off at Thirty-Fourth Street to go back to the office, though. Instead, I stayed on the B all the way to Broadway-Lafayette. SoHo. Juniper Designs' main office on West Broadway and Prince.

I would show Dylan the photos in person. I wanted to see his face. Know where we stood. And maybe if I saw him, I'd know how I felt too.

Juniper Designs was an open, airy space, with their signature furniture scattered around the large SoHo loft space. Dylan's office was at the back, in the far right corner. Naturally.

Dylan half-rose from his chair, then sat back down, making a sweeping gesture between me and the two other people in the room. "Beth, Fritz, this Sa— Samantha Lilly." The stutter was so smoothly covered, nobody but me could possibly know he'd been about to say Saffron. "She's a junior architect with Alvarez."

Beth, an elegant older woman perched on the low-slung modernist couch, gave me a look. Her narrow legs were tightly crossed and her gaze conveyed authority. "You're working on the storefront?"

"I just came from the Seventy-Second Street site. I thought you'd like to see." I gestured with my pocket camera.

Fritz held his hand out. He could have been Dylan's older brother, with mussed dark hair and cheekbones so sharp they'd cut you if you came too close.

I glanced at Dylan. He nodded, all business. So much for a tête-à-tête.

"It would be better to view the images on the computer screen." But I handed over the camera.

Fritz thumbed through them fast, then handed the camera to Beth. Dylan came around the desk and looked over her shoulder. Nobody said a word.

When they finished, Dylan handed the camera back to me. His fingers brushed against mine, sending a jolt of recognition through me. *This touch. This man.*

Yes.

His gaze caught mine briefly. The hunger was back but banked before he turned back to his colleagues with raised eyebrows. "Told you." He crossed his arms and leaned back against the desk.

Beth turned to me, her lips quirked. "I want to hear what our young architect thinks of the space."

Me? I looked at Dylan for help, but he wasn't giving me anything. Some friend. "I'm only here dropping off the pictures."

"You don't have an opinion?" Dylan's voice was deceptively soft. "Unusual." Yup, soft but with a hidden bite.

You couldn't get fired for having an unpopular opinion, could you?

Of course you could. And though Fernando was currently amused with me, if I screwed things up with Juniper, I wouldn't be so funny anymore.

Still, I wasn't going to prevaricate. "It would be a disaster. The light's all wrong. It makes the space feel oppressive. And there's no real freight entrance. To move furniture in and out, you'd have to reconfigure the back entirely, and I'm not sure you could get a variance for the freight entrance you'd need. The community board up there is prickly, I hear."

"So you're saying it's not a flexible space. It's not open to change." Dylan's words definitely had a bite to them. Why? I thought we were friends. I thought Friday night brought us closer. What was this about? What did he expect from me? *Open to change,* what did that even mean?

But I persevered as if we were talking about the potential storefront, not our personal lives. "There are better choices. Even if they're not quite as convenient for you to roll out of bed and be in the showroom five minutes later."

Fritz and Beth gave me startled glances, and I realized my faux pas. There was no way some random underling at Alvarez would know where a top executive at Juniper lived.

"I mean, I heard you live around there."

He gave me an approving look. "You heard right. But I wasn't in favor of the site."

I exhaled, but quietly, so they couldn't tell I'd felt my entire body go from DEFCON Five back to normal. Thank God. I hadn't just killed my career.

"So we find another space." Beth turned to me. "Where do you suggest?"

"I heard the big pharmacy on Eighty-Sixth is shutting its doors. There was some talk of Banana Republic moving in, but I don't think it came to anything."

"Get up there, take some shots for us. Report back." She turned to Dylan. "Now, about the Jurgen chair, here's a mock-up, but I think it's not going to work with the wood." She tapped on her tablet screen and turned it to face him.

Clearly dismissed, I turned to go, feeling perversely disappointed.

I didn't go back uptown to take more pictures. Dylan's bossy compatriot could wait until tomorrow. I had other work to do, after all, and a job that didn't involve all Dylan, all the time.

Which didn't make it easier to block the man from my thoughts. Back at my station at Alvarez and Associates, I chewed on the end of my mechanical pencil and stared at the Newark building drawings one more time. I'd managed to put in bathrooms and even doors this time, but it was flat and boring. An office complex like thousands of others. It needed curved wood, track lighting, warmth.

I opened my email and wrote a note to Dylan. *Are you angry at me?*

Two minutes later, my mail program chimed. *Why would I be? You presented a clear case against the site.*

I responded. *That crack about not being open to change.*

The response came sooner this time. *This would be easier if I had your phone number.*

After everything, it seemed ridiculous that he

didn't have it. Who was I kidding? I gave him my phone number.

My cell phone rang immediately. Rudy shot me a glance. I set my pencil down and answered, heading down the row of drafting tables toward the exit and that quiet spot by the elevator bank. "I just didn't understand all the digs. I guess I don't know where we stand now. *Friend.*"

"Are we friends, then?"

"You thought so Friday night. Or do you not remember?"

"I'm a maudlin drunk. Completely untrustworthy. Friendship, as I know it, is an equal proposition. I spill, you spill. You comfort, I comfort. But you won't allow that, or if you do, it's for such a short moment, and then you pull back. You won't let anyone in."

I leaned against the wall for support. Fernando walked past with a group of senior architects. They didn't see me.

I used to like to be invisible. I used to prefer it that way. What was happening to me?

My phone beeped. Another call. I pulled the phone away from my ear to check. My aunt. She never called me. It must be important.

"Can you hold on a second?"

"Samantha." He sounded exasperated.

"I'll be right back. I swear. I'm not running away."

I clicked over. "Aunt Margaret?"

"He's gone."

I blinked in confusion. Her five-year-old son, Colin? "When did you last see him? Did his school call you?"

"School? What? No. Papa. Gramps."

I shook my head even though she couldn't see me. "But he's not that mobile, is he? Didn't his nurse notice?"

Her breath caught. "No. *Gone*. An hour ago. He had a stroke last night, and we brought him to the hospital. I was going to call you this morning, but…" She choked. "He's gone. He's just…gone."

I held the phone against my ear. Stood on pale blue tile, leaned against a cream-painted semigloss wall. Breathed.

"But I talked to him a few days ago." The night I didn't meet Dylan. The night I saw him at the Greenpoint Pleasures party. "A week and a half ago. He sounded fine." Except that he didn't. Confused, disoriented, distant.

"I know. I *know*."

Oh God, I'd left Dylan hanging on the other line. "I have to go. I'll call you later. I'll come down tonight."

I switched back to Dylan. "I'm sorry. Where were we?"

He was gone.

I cradled the phone in my hand, staring at the elevator bank. Lit numbers ticking off floors. The closest elevator was stuck on the fourth floor. Maybe someone was having trouble getting on. Maybe an old person, someone who moved slowly.

I pictured my grandfather's wrinkled face, his thin lips, his eyebrows and the way they tilted up at the edges. Gone.

Jeanine offered to drive down for the weekend with me. I told her I'd take Amtrak to Philadelphia on Tuesday and a bus out to my aunt's house. Besides, I was fine. I hadn't cried once.

I *was* fine, by all objective measures. I ate, I slept, I took regular showers. My aunt Margaret put me to work writing Gramps's obituary, calling the people she hadn't yet told, and arranging for flowers and a buffet.

And then came the funeral. I still didn't cry, but I wasn't okay anymore.

The minister's speech was short and to the point. Gramps would have liked it.

As people got up and spoke about Gramps, they painted a portrait of a man I would have liked to have known. A man I caught glimpses of over the years. They said he loved woodworking. And yes, I remembered the way the power saw would shake the small house at seven a.m. on Saturday morning. They said he was passionate about current events. Yes, I remembered him cursing at the news every night religiously at eleven p.m. They said he was a devoted husband and father. I didn't know what they meant by that.

My eyes felt sandy. Dry.

My aunt stood. Solemn in her ill-cut black suit, she made her way to the podium. "Pops was a good man who lost too much. When my mother died ten years ago, he withstood that like the stoic he was. But my sister's death five years before that, it changed him. Made him pull into his shell like a turtle. He rarely laughed after Laura's death, and hugged the rest of us less often. Still, though, he loved us in his way. As best as he was able. And he took my sister's daughter into his home to raise." She gestured toward me. "A kindness."

A kindness. She made me sound like some random waif, not family.

I stood. I guess she assumed I was coming up to the podium to say a few words about the dearly departed, because she stepped away from the mic, making room. But I shook my head, feeling a buzzing in my ears. I felt dizzy.

I walked down the aisle toward the door. People watched me go, then looked away as I caught their gazes.

I opened the door to the vestibule, walked through, opened the outer door, and emerged outside. The cold air smacked my cheeks. I wrapped my arms around my torso and stared across the parking lot toward the bare fingers of the trees along the highway.

I breathed deep of the cold air, sucked it in. It wasn't enough. It didn't clear my head, didn't ease my heart.

Without consciously thinking it through, I fished my phone out of my coat pocket.

Dylan answered on the first ring. "Samantha. Do you have shots of the Eighty-Sixth Street location? You can email them to me." He sounded curt. As cold as the sharp breeze now toying with my hair.

"I'm not at work."

"Then why…?"

"I didn't call you back Monday because…" I exhaled a cloud of steam into the cold air. "Because my aunt was on the other line. She called to tell me my grandfather had died. And I thought about calling you after that, to let you know, but…"

I could hear his breath catch. "I see. Yes. I do see." He paused. "Are you—where are you from, anyway? Are you there?"

"Pennsylvania. Half an hour west of Philadelphia." I don't know why I added that part. Next, I was going to give him directions. "The funeral is this morning. Now, in fact."

"You're at the funeral?" His voice was a rumble in my ear. In my chest. A comfort.

"It's in the church. I'm on the front steps. They're super white, like someone bleaches them once a week. The church is ultramodern, very clean. I don't think my grandfather came here. He wasn't into organized religion. That was more my grandmother's thing. He said it was a lot of fuss and bother."

Dylan was quiet. I felt like I was talking to myself. "I should go."

"Back inside?"

"I might miss the exciting part." A coloratura's ethereal aria rose from inside the church. "Too late."

"How are you doing with this? I mean, obviously you're fine, because you always are. You were born that way." The smile in his voice warmed me. "But this is not an easy thing. It would be okay not to be fine."

There was a huge pile of brown leaves along the nearest edge of the parking lot, the only evidence of anything organic in this immaculate setting. On impulse, I walked over to it. "I didn't cry in there."

"Why am I not surprised?" It should have been a mean thing to say, but his tone was affectionate.

"I shouldn't have called. I'm sorry I interrupted your Saturday."

"I'm glad you did." He hesitated. I could hear the almost-words. Then he said, "Why *did* you call me? And not your roommate, I mean. Or did you call her too?"

I hadn't even thought about calling her. "Just you." When I reached the leaf pile, I stomped my foot down. The leaves crackled and settled underfoot. "I wanted you to know why I disappeared like that." I kicked the pile, and a few leaves scattered. "Besides, we're friends, aren't we?"

He was quiet for a moment. "Yes. We are."

I picked up a leaf. It was brittle. When I crumpled it in my palm, it turned to dust. "My grandfather liked woodworking. Like you, except he wasn't as inventive. He made a violin once, though."

Dylan whistled. "That takes some skill. Did he play?"

"Badly." I smiled. I couldn't help it. I could picture my grandfather, his white head bowed, perched on a stool in the den, running the bow against the violin strings in more of a caterwaul than a sustained musical note.

"My grandfather played the accordion."

"Was he good?"

"It sounds like a cat fight. No, more like cat gang warfare. Roving bands of cat bandits duking it out with the cops. So no. He wasn't." Dylan's tone was intimate, amused. I relaxed for the first time since I'd gotten here.

We kept talking, his voice a soothing anchor in this foreign yet familiar territory. I crushed leaves and walked the perimeter of the parking lot as we shared stories about our grandparents. Dylan told me about his father too. He'd learned woodcraft from him. They'd never talked much, but they'd worked side by side in the converted garage that served as his dad's workshop, trading tools. When his father showed him how to hold the saw blade so it wouldn't hurt him, or showed him the proper way to level a board, Dylan had felt closer to him than any other time.

I thought about my grandfather, about his silences. He'd given me books. Old, dusty tomes with red leather binding, *Robinson Crusoe* and *10,000 Leagues Under the Sea*. Adventure stories. I'd thought he was tacitly saying he wished I was a boy, but maybe not. Maybe that was his way of saying he loved me.

I didn't remember much about my father at all. I told Dylan this.

"How old were you when he died?"

"Seven. Old enough to have some memories, you'd think."

"Memory's a funny thing."

We talked until the mourners started filing out of the church. I caught my aunt's glare, visible across the large parking lot. I felt caught, like a schoolgirl ditching gym class to smoke in the recess yard.

"I have to go. Funeral's over. Thanks for listening."

"Any time. I'm…" He hesitated. "I'm glad you called."

"Me too." And I was. Maybe Dylan could be my friend after all.

I slipped the phone into my jacket pocket and smiled at my young cousin, Colin, who tackled my legs with great enthusiasm. "That was the boringest ceremony ever. How do we even know Gramps is in that box, anyway? Maybe they put another body in there instead of his, to fool us. Maybe he escaped and ran away."

I squeezed him. "Maybe so. Come on, let's go give the unknown stranger a proper burial, shall we?"

After a simple ceremony in a verdant cemetery, we returned to the house for a reception. My aunt put on classical music with a heavy violin section. Gramps would have approved.

After everyone left, Margaret disappeared into the garage and came back with a cardboard box, not much larger than a shoe box. "If it's too big to carry on the train, I'll mail it to you. I kept some things, but as Laura's daughter, I felt you should have some too."

When I got to the guest room, I opened the box.

Then immediately closed it again.

Then opened it to peek inside again.

The box was filled with memorabilia. In that brief moment, I saw the handle of a carefully wrapped porcelain teacup I remembered her using. Letters written in spidery script on yellowed pages with embossed curlicues at the corners. A photo of me at age two curled in my mother's lap. One of her at five, bare-assed as she ran along a narrow strip of beach.

I closed it again and hugged it to my chest.

The room felt claustrophobic. Dresser, nightstand, framed photograph of trees, white bedspread. It could have been a hotel room, it was so impersonal.

There was a night train back to New York. I could be in Penn Station before midnight. Back to my funky patchwork quilt and my funky patchwork living room and my funky unconventional roommate. And if I thought of Dylan, imagined seeing him, that wasn't the whole thing or the only thing or even a realistic thing. Mostly, I wanted to leave. To go back to my own life.

I called a cab and left a note on the kitchen counter apologizing to Margaret. Telling her I'd call in a few days. Telling her to give the kids hugs for me.

She'd been in college when I came to live with her parents. We'd never gotten to know each other, not really. Our lives were so different. She and Brian probably only did it in the missionary position. In the dark. Under the covers. With the door locked. She didn't take risks, not ever. And she had no sense of humor.

But she was family. The only one I had. So I added a postscript saying I loved her. Whatever that meant.

Chapter Thirteen

The subway station had a notice outside the turnstile saying the G train wasn't running overnight. Which meant I was screwed. I could take the L, but the station was a mile away from my apartment, and I was lugging a heavy suitcase while carrying an unwieldy cardboard box.

Or I could spring for a taxi. The cab stand outside Penn Station was swarming with people coming from a concert at Madison Square Garden, so I walked two blocks uptown along Seventh Avenue and hailed cabs until my arm felt like it might fall off.

Finally, one pulled up at the curb. The driver popped the trunk and got out to help me with my bags. Thank God.

"Where are you going?" His Middle East accent was thick with new-to-America uncertainty.

I hesitated. I should go home. It was too late to go anywhere else. And yet... "The Upper West Side."

As Times Square flashed past, I called Dylan. His phone rang through to voice mail.

It was midnight. What was I doing?

Same thing I'd done the first time I went to see him. I was flying without a net. Stepping outside my own personal rules.

Riding in the backseat of a cab heading up Broadway toward the only person I could imagine giving me comfort tonight.

He wasn't home. Or, at least, he wasn't answering the doorman's call.

"Can you try again?" I stood in the ornate lobby, clutching my cardboard box stuffed with painful memories, my suitcase leaning against my shin. What now? Find an all-night diner and wait out the subway changeover? Hope for a cabbie willing to take me over the bridge? A car service?

My chest hurt.

The doorman gave me a kindly look. "I'm sorry. Why don't you sit for a bit?" He gestured toward the leatherette bench against the far wall.

Before I could gather my things and trudge over there, the front door swung open and Dylan walked in with a woman. She was imposingly tall, with her dark hair upswept and her makeup perfectly applied. She was half-turned toward him, and they were both laughing.

Somehow I hadn't pictured this.

Nothing for it. I smiled. Fake and wide. "There you are."

Dylan stopped laughing. "Samantha?"

The woman craned her head around, gazing at me

with annoyance.

"I thought I'd stop by and say hi. But you're busy, so I'll go. No problem. I'll talk to you soon." I clutched the box against my chest and felt around for the suitcase handle.

"No. Wait." He stepped forward and took the box out of my arms. "You should come up and—" Belatedly, he glanced over at his companion. "Can we take a rain check on drinks?" Was it wrong that I was pleased to see how much of an afterthought she was?

"Of course." Her smile was faker than mine had been. "Family takes precedence."

"Samantha's a friend."

Her smile froze in place. "Even better." She brushed a kiss on his cheek and gave me a condescending wave, then rushed outside.

"I don't want to cock-block you. I'll go."

"Don't be ridiculous. Rochelle is a friend from high school. She's in town for the week from California."

And she expected to get in your pants tonight. But I followed him to the elevator shaft, smiling to myself because he didn't act disappointed in the least.

He pressed the elevator button and turned to me. "Are you okay? I thought you were staying in Pennsylvania until Monday. You said you'd call me, not…"

"Show up on your doorstep like an orphan from a Dickens story?"

The elevator door opened. We stepped on, my wheeled suitcase following us. The doors closed, and we rose up. Those mirrored walls, those mahogany strips along the edges. They kept reflecting intense moments in my life. The first time I came here, wearing a red corset and vibrating with tension and anticipation. The second time, with Dylan after the hospital, steamy and ultimately thwarted. Now? The mirror reflected travel-worn me and scruffy, jeans-clad, so-familiar Dylan.

I met his gaze in the mirror. "I'm sorry to barge in on you."

"Stop apologizing. I'm glad you're here." He sounded sincere, but his breath had a wine taste to it, and the way that woman had been leaning in, well…

I gripped the metal handle of the suitcase. "I was tired, and they're doing track work on the G, which is the closest to my apartment." *And I wanted to see you.* "You've never been there, have you?"

"Are you inviting me over?"

I pictured him sitting on the floor, eating pizza and tossing a handful of poker chips on our unconventional coffee table. "Not tonight, but yeah. Why not?"

His smile crinkled his eyes. "I'd like that."

The elevator door opened, and we walked down the hallway to his apartment, my suitcase trundling behind us like an unusually obedient toddler.

He ushered me inside. "Have you eaten?"

"Hors d'oeuvres at the reception. Lasagna for dinner. Microwaved hot dog on the train."

"You had an appetite for all that?"

"A few bites of the hot dog. It was pretty bad." I realized I was gripping the metal handle of the suitcase as if I was planning to leave. So I slid it back into the suitcase frame and went over to the couch. I was here. I might as well *be* here.

Dylan settled on the couch next to me and set the box on the floor. "What happened, really?"

I hesitated.

He took my hand in both of his. "Samantha."

I cocked my head, questioning.

He dropped my hand, as if realizing he shouldn't be so intimate. I could feel the reverberations of that electric warmth like an echo up my arm.

"My aunt gave me this. And I couldn't stay after that. Here, see." I knelt by the box, opened it, and pulled out the first thing my fingers touched, which turned out to be a blue ribbon for horsemanship with my mother's name down the side.

My mother was a horsewoman? I looked at the year and did the math. A horse-mad preteen girl. The ribbon color was faded except for the slice of fabric right along a crease, where it was still vivid aqua.

I put it back in the box and rummaged around again, pulling out a sheaf of photos. I handed them to Dylan. "My grandfather had them in his room in the nursing home. My brusque, dry-as-dust grandfather had a hidden sentimental streak. Go figure."

He took the pictures and leafed through them. When he was done, he held out his hand for more. I gave him another sheaf, and we looked through them together. They were in poor condition. Many were stained or creased, or their edges were ragged. Had it been my mother's negligence, or my grandfather's?

"Your mother laughed a lot, it seems."

"Until she didn't." In the photo, she was standing in a field, her head thrown back, her mouth open. A completely unselfconscious belly laugh. My father looked on from the side of the frame, smiling at her pleasure. They were so young.

Dylan flipped through the stack of pictures and asked questions as he went. I started telling him stories, and all kinds of memories came gushing out. Like water from a faucet I'd kept shut off for a decade —rusty at first but growing stronger and cleaner the more it flowed.

For the first time in a long time, I remembered what was good and fun and happy about my mother.

She loved the beach, the woods, the mountains. Reveled in being outdoors.

She loved my father desperately and would make elaborate meals every weekend, whether for the three of us or for a crowd of people. She was lovely and giddy and charming and sweet.

And only had eyes for my father. Every photo of the two of them showed her gazing up at him. Every photo he took showed her looking lovingly into the camera. I commented on this to Dylan, and he nodded. "I noticed that too. It looks like he defined her world."

Somewhere along the way, Dylan and I both slid down to the floor, our backs against the couch. I leaned into his side, and he put his arm around me. It felt so natural, I didn't question it.

I stared down at a photo of my mother and me together. She was staring off into the distance. I was looking up at her, yearning for something I'd never have.

Dylan contemplated it. "You were a loving kid."

"A lot of good it did me."

"It's not about that, not always. It's about who you are, deep down." He pulled out another photo. It depicted me gazing into the camera, dressed up as a pirate, with a smile that lit up my little face. "This is you."

I traced the white crease that ran through the image, slicing across my childhood likeness's sun-dappled arm and vest. "Thank you."

"For what?"

"For being here. For letting me crash in your apartment. For looking at all this with me." I gestured toward the dusty photos scattered across the rug. "Helping me face the scary monsters."

"My pleasure." He brushed a stray hair out of my face. "I mean that, Samantha."

We sat like that for a long heartbeat, staring at each other. Then I set the photo down on the carpet and leaned forward. Deliberately, giving him time to pull away.

He didn't pull away.

It was different, this kiss. Softer. Like *hello* and *welcome*. It made my body melt, a subtle hunger, yearning for more. Lips and tongues and short sharp breaths. I caressed the back of his neck, running my fingertips across the tiny short hairs, pulling him closer. He moaned deep in his throat—

And pulled away. "We can't." He rubbed his cheeks vigorously.

I sat back. "Right. That woman, your high school friend. I shouldn't have…"

Dylan looked baffled. "Oh, Rochelle? No, that's— she's—" He hesitated. "I haven't, not since you. And I thought I should. But I was already having second thoughts. I'd decided to share a bottle of wine, kiss her on the cheek, and send her on her way."

"Oh." The unfamiliar warmth in my chest was relief. "But then why not?"

"Because you're not ready for a real relationship. And I'm not interested in anything else." He sagged back against the couch. "And because a friend doesn't take advantage of another friend's grief."

I smoothed his cheek with the back of my hand, relishing the roughness of his stubble against my skin. "What if I want you to take advantage?"

He put his hand over mine, stopping me. "It's not up to you." He pulled me against him. "Stop being seductive. It won't work." The bulge in his jeans gave the lie to his words, but that wasn't what he meant.

I pulled away. "I should go."

"Go where? It's two a.m. Stay."

"But…" I gestured between us. My hair fell forward, shielding my face.

He drew it back, tucked it behind my ears, just as he had before. An achingly tender gesture. "I think I can manage to keep my hands off you. Can you promise the same?"

I sucked in my bottom lip. God, he was hot. Disheveled, his dress shirt wrinkled from slouching against the couch, his five o'clock shadow more like a dark scrub across his cheeks and chin, his hair in clumps.

Desire snaked up my spine. I wanted to use his body to help me forget. No, to center me, to connect, to feel alive and whole and…

He was right. This was getting too complicated. Sex wasn't merely sex anymore. If it ever had been.

I gathered the scattered photos, piled them neatly, and squared off the stack. "Where do I sleep? Here, on the couch?"

"Or you can crash in my bed. It's king-size, after all. Plenty of room." He got up and headed into his bedroom without glancing back.

By the time I got to the doorway of his room, Dylan was peeling off his jeans. "I'm assuming you have nightclothes in your luggage, but if not, you can borrow a T-shirt."

"Are you sure this is a good idea?"

"After the day you've had, I don't like the idea of you spending the night alone on the couch. But it's up to you." Dylan unbuttoned his shirt and removed it. Now he only wore loose-fitting boxers. I tried not to look at the play of muscles along his back and legs as he folded the edge of the comforter down, revealing deep blue flannel sheets. The sheets had been pale gray the night I'd met him. I remembered straddling him on those sheets. I remembered kisses, caresses, feeling him move inside me, a feeling of completeness…

I fled to the living room.

The couch was so plush, I sank into it. Like riding the tide in a saltwater pond, I floated, semisubmerged. Dylan had given me a soft blanket, but I kicked it off. It made me feel like I was in a suffocating cocoon.

I stared up at the ceiling. First, I sleepily watched the play of light from outside, then I gradually shifted my attention to the crown molding. It was an unusual pattern: geometric shapes, squares and triangles in repeating patterns. Staring up through the earliest-morning dawn gloom, I could make out the drips and globs of a careless paint job. Too bad. It was probably a good hardwood underneath.

This wasn't working. It was after six a.m. and I was nowhere near sleep. Too aware of my incongruous presence in Dylan's silent living room, with its hand-carved chair and elegant side table. Dylan's handiwork, his presence in absentia. And then there were my grandfather's photos, stacked neatly next to the cardboard box I'd lugged all the way from Pennsylvania. Two wineglasses rested on the side table, the few drops of wine remaining looking like congealed bloodstains in the dark.

I went down the short hall and peeked into the bedroom. Dylan was fast asleep, sprawled across his enormous bed. He'd put on sweatpants, but he'd thrown the cover off. The sweet curve of his back and ridge of shoulder blades were gently illuminated by the brightening dawn. I could picture going over to the bed, the mattress settling under my weight, and caressing the revealed skin. He'd be half-asleep, with morning wood. He wouldn't be thinking about *shouldn't* and *complicated*. It would be easy to seduce him.

My body responded instantly to the idea. So easy. Shut off my brain and fuck him senseless.

So easy to sabotage a fragile, precious friendship in a single stupid maneuver.

I retreated to the kitchen, where I poured myself a glass of water. Holding the blue-rimmed Mexican tumbler, I walked back out through the dining area to the living room area. There should be an arch separating the two spaces.

Sure enough, when I went to the spot, I saw a patchwork of short floorboards where the half-wall must have been. An arch with built-ins, painted cream with darker colors in the nooks to make a few well-chosen small sculptures stand out. Yes, that would work. I grabbed a pen from the kitchen counter and the only paper I could find—a takeout menu from the local Japanese restaurant—and started sketching. If the arch went here and the wall dividing the crying-out-for-a-remodel kitchen from the dining room were gone, then…

Yes, that could work, and then…

The sky lightened, which was good, because I could see my work better.

The fireplace was a problem. Someone had blocked it up somewhere along the way, though you could see the original ornate woodwork running up the sides. But it had no mantel.

I set my pen down and went over to investigate. It was behind Dylan's carved wood chair, so I tugged on that to move it out of the way. The chair was heavier than it looked. I had to pick it up to get it past the edge of the carpet. It dropped back down with a loud thunk.

Ah yes. I ran my hand along the fireplace. The mantel had been along the wall here. The current wall would have to be reinforced, but if you used a lighter wood for a new mantel…

"Decided to rearrange my furniture in the middle of the night?" Dylan stood by the couch, blinking sleepily as he rubbed a hand over his stubble.

I hastily pulled my hand away from the plaster, as if I'd been caught caressing his skin. "Thinking about what could be done with this place if you wanted to put in the money."

"You can't exactly move that wall, you know. It's

an outside wall. Might get chilly. And wet, when it rains."

I frowned at him. "I was trying to see how hard it would be to add a new mantel. If you want to restore this fireplace, which maybe you don't."

"Hmm." He headed toward the kitchen but paused when he saw the takeout menu with my scribbles all over it. He picked it up. "You've been at this awhile. Did you get any sleep?"

I suppressed a yawn. "Some. I think."

He glanced over at the open cardboard box. "Too many ghosts?"

"Something like that."

He went into the kitchen and started up the coffeemaker.

I followed him in. "I should get out of your hair. Let you get on with your day." The coffeemaker gurgled, and the dark, rich scent wafted up. "Is there enough for me to have a cup before I go?"

"Of course." He picked up the former takeout menu and looked from it to the space around us. "Can you explain this? What does this mean?" He pointed to the lines I'd made sketching in the arch.

So I explained. We sat in the breakfast nook, coffee mugs in hand and toasted bagels slathered with cream cheese on plates in front of us, and I gestured around the room and talked about the history of architecture design on the Upper West Side and what this place must have looked like a hundred years ago. Dylan leaned forward, his coffee forgotten. He asked intelligent questions. I answered as best I could, hoping my memory from grad school classes was accurate, and talked more. I felt dizzy with exhaustion, my eyes sticky from lack of sleep. The room was hazy and soft, but his face was sharply in focus.

At some point, I realized I'd stopped talking and was staring at him. His eyes. So brown. So perceptive. So deep. His eyebrows. So fuzzy. So dark. His refined nose. Aquiline, that was the word. Roman. A strong nose.

"Samantha?"

I startled. I'd been drifting. Half-asleep. Dreaming of Dylan's nose. "Yes. I'm here." I rubbed my face vigorously. "I need more coffee." I took a big gulp of the now-lukewarm liquid.

"What you need is a nap."

"Yeah. I'll go home and crash. Get out of your way."

"What do you think I'm planning to do today that's so important you have to leave?" He picked up the dishes and took them to the sink.

"Businessman stuff. Big fancy entrepreneur stuff. Or maybe you'll call that hot chick from high school if she's still in town."

"Should I? Do you want to meet her?"

I shrugged, trying to look nonchalant. "We're friends. You won't sleep with me. You should get laid."

"Maybe I don't want to simply get laid. Maybe I want more."

"You're the marrying kind, aren't you? Not fling material. Too bad. You don't know better. It's in your DNA."

He did something that surprised me then. He came over and kissed my forehead. "It's in yours too, if you'd only stop fighting it." He took me by the hand and tugged me to a standing position. "I have a proposition for you."

"*Do* you?" I raised my eyebrows suggestively.

He shook his head at me. "I want to hire you."

"Didn't we do that already?" I leaned against him. Tired. So. Very. Tired. But if he wanted me, I'd drink more coffee and make a go of it. I'd do that for him. And for me, admittedly. He was great in bed, after all. And oh boy, I was delirious with fatigue.

"No, to remodel my apartment. To supervise the work. Draw up the plans. A side project. We can clear it with your boss, if you like."

"Seriously?" I pulled back to look at him.

"I like your ideas. And maybe I like the idea of having you around more." He tucked me firmly into his side and walked me to the bedroom. "First, though, you need to sleep. I'll stay fully clothed, I promise."

"No sex?"

"No sex."

"Bummer." But I went with him.

He made a surprisingly good bolster. He leaned back against the headboard, paging through his tablet computer while I curled up under that lovely comforter. Listening to his breathing, feeling the radiant warmth of his body, I fell asleep and slept soundly for the first time in ages. If this was friendship, I could live with that.

When I woke up, I was alone in the big bed. Cold winter sunlight bathed the room in shades of bluish white. I should get up. Should thank Dylan and head home. Instead, I snuggled deeper under the comforter and fell into a light doze.

The door opened, and Dylan came in with a tray of food. An extravagant tray, with pâté and strawberries and stinky cheese. I sat up. This was worth waking up for.

He set the tray on the bed and sat next to me. "I thought you might be hungry." He picked up a strawberry and bit into it. "Okay, I confess, I was hungry and thought it would be rude to eat alone." He grinned at me and picked up another strawberry, proffering it.

I took a bite, savoring the juicy tartness. "Mmm." I sliced off a piece of pâté and slathered it on a cracker. "You're spoiling me. How can I go back to my mundane apartment with my psych-grad-student call-girl roommate after this?"

"I'm a bad influence." His dimples popped. Such a delicious smile.

Something had shifted between us yet again. I leaned across the tray and gave him a quick kiss on the mouth, then pulled away, embarrassed. "Uh, was that okay? Friends kiss each other, don't they?"

His mouth twitched. "Not my friends. We play racquetball."

We ate and flirted until the tray was nothing but crumbs and balled-up napkins, then Dylan set it aside and flicked on the TV, leaning back against the headboard to watch. I should go. I should get up, put my shoes on, and leave.

I snuggled against his warmth. He smelled like clean laundry and clean skin. My heart felt as full as my stomach. I felt warm and comfortable and like I belonged. Like I fit. I sighed and said the first thing that popped into my head, entirely uncensored. "I love you."

He stiffened.

Panic flooded my body, sharp and painful. I

sprang away from him. "I mean, I love *this*. This is awesome. You've been great, a real friend, and I appreciate it."

I bolted into the living room. The words, those words. Dylan had frozen, no response, and oh God, I couldn't— Love was—I couldn't go there. Couldn't mean it. The churning in my stomach said *but you did, you meant it*. My head pounded, my chest hurt. I couldn't think straight. I had to go. Right now.

My stuff. Where was my stuff?

I grabbed a pair of jeans out of my suitcase, zipped it shut, shoved my feet into my shoes, grabbed my coat...

Dylan came out of the bedroom. "Do you mean it?"

I shrugged my coat on. "Sure, I meant it. I love everything you've done for me."

"Samantha."

"I overslept. I have to get going. Get ready for work tomorrow. I've got a list of chores a mile long. Thanks for everything, you're a good friend, see you around."

And I fled, my heart pounding like the bass line at a rave, a pure shot of fear racing through me.

Love him? Had I said that? Did I mean it? *Could* I mean it?

Chapter Fourteen

I snagged a seat on the subway despite the Sunday crowd heading downtown. My unkempt hair and wild-eyed expression probably made people wary. Give the crazy lady a seat so she doesn't fall apart and smash into us.

I love you.

The cadence in my head, those three words over and over, acted as a counterpoint to the grind and rush of the subway through the tunnel.

My mother, crying for a year nonstop. Gramps, stone silent in the wake of her death.

The voice in my head was Dylan's. *It's who you are, deep down.*

The voice in my head was mine, over and over. *I love you I love you I love you.*

I stumbled off the B, up the steps and back down, changing platforms. Changing trains. Changing my life story. Heading where?

An E was waiting, thankfully. No seat this time. I hugged the pole tight. Images flashed through my brain like a slide show of photographs I couldn't block out. And they were all of the same man.

Dylan, the first time I saw him, toweling himself dry after a shower. That dark hungry gaze that I now knew was part pain, part yearning for something better. Something mutual and real.

Dylan, after the first time we'd made love, because that was what it was even then. When I'd hung up on Persephone and focused entirely on him. His look of surprised revelation, of openness and delight.

Dylan when he'd stopped at my desk, the moment he found out that Saffron was Samantha, his shock scaldingly potent. And yet he didn't tear me to shreds in front of my boss, didn't make me feel small and stupid. Instead, he showed me with his body how much I meant to him. Showed me with his passion. I just couldn't see it. Not then.

The burly guy next to me started singing. Random words, blurted aloud. Singing along to words only he could hear. "Oh baby," and then silence. "I miss you like a gunshot wound, yeah, baby," and then he quieted again, nodding to the beat emanating from his tiny white earbuds.

Miss you like a gunshot wound.

Yesterday at the funeral, Dylan was the one I'd called. The only one I'd wanted to hear from.

I bowed my head so far down it almost hit my knees. Beside me, Singing Guy rapped, "Baby, you're my heart on a string," which didn't even make sense, but it still resonated in my clenched gut.

Across from me, a tiny kid stood on the long blue

bench, peering out the window. Her braids tumbled past her hoodie. Her mother put her hand out to prevent her daughter from falling, though the woman never looked up from her book. She sensed the need and reacted.

A visceral memory: my mother buckling me into a car seat. Handing me a candy bar, half-unwrapped. Taking care of me.

By the next pole, a teenage boy with scruff that was trying too hard to be a goatee chatted up a pretty girl who swung her school backpack by one shoulder strap. She smiled shyly up at him, her heart in her eyes.

My heart on a string. My heart as a pull toy. Dylan had my heart, dammit. But I'd walked away from him so many times now, he'd be an idiot to believe me. And I'd walked away this morning—no, I'd run away, I'd fled, I'd bolted like he was about to devour me, engulf me, demolish me, and—

The train lurched to a halt, and the doors slid open. Greenpoint Avenue. My stop.

I walked off the train and headed down the platform, pulling my heart—or rather, my rolling suitcase. When I emerged from the station, I found myself among the bodegas and dry cleaners and little Polish bakeries of central Greenpoint. Home had never looked so dreary.

At some point, I must have started to cry, but I didn't know it until I tasted the salt on my lips. I wiped my cheek with the back of my hand and kept going. Down the street, turn right, down the next block, cross the street, keep going. No longer numb. My heart on a string. My love floating in the East River, the gulf between us.

Dylan had rebuffed my kiss. He'd stiffened when I said the words. He might be the marrying kind, but would he trust his heart to me? Could he trust me?

And what then, if he did?

My mother, looking at my father like he was the center of her universe. My mother the zombie after his death.

That wasn't me. Couldn't be me.

Panic clogged my throat. I gasped, stuttered in my stride. Walking down the street, breathing hard, pulling the damned suitcase behind me. The box of memories clutched to my chest. The box of proof. Love enveloped you. Love blessed you and comforted you and thrilled you and gave you a sense of belonging and rightness until love dropped dead of a heart attack and killed all that was strong in you.

But the thought of never seeing Dylan again, of walking away from him for real this time, it felt worse. Like a hole in my gut. Like a bottomless pit. *Love you like a gunshot wound.*

It was too late. I was doomed. I loved him.

I was crying so hard I couldn't see.

By the time I got to the narrow apartment building, I was drooping, looking down at the sidewalk, clutching the cardboard box and dragging the suitcase. A wanderer, a waif, a wreck, dripping tears down my chin.

Which is how it happened. I walked into a human wall where the front stoop should have been.

Dylan stood there, in my doorway. *My doorway.* Here. In Greenpoint.

Under an elegant wool coat, he still wore the sweatpants he'd had on when I left his apartment an hour ago.

"You're crying." He took the box from me and set it down on the ground. "Why?"

Because I love you. Because it hurts.

He brushed the wetness from my cheeks with his thumbs. "Because of me?"

I nodded. "If I let myself care about you…" I swallowed, tasting salt.

His fingers stilled, touching my cheeks and chin. Framing my face. "Do you?"

"So much. Too much." I shook my head, a sharp shake, dislodging his fingers. "But if I let you in and you leave me, I don't know how I'll—"

He put his finger over my mouth, gently shushing

me. "First of all, I won't leave."

I brushed his fingers aside. "You can't promise that. You can't know."

"I can. I do. I've known for seven months. You shook me out of my self-pity and helped me remember how to relish life. Being with you was a revelation."

I almost said *that's sex,* but he stopped me.

"It wasn't the striptease or the sex, though they were both…well…" His eyes tilted up, his mouth twitched. The warmth in his expression thawed places inside me I didn't know were so cold before. "But mostly it was *you.* The way you sauntered into my living room and took over, even though it was obvious you were nervous as hell. The way you revealed something of your own pain to me that night even though you didn't have to. Because you knew I needed to feel less alone."

He smiled fully now, and it was beautiful the way it lit his face. "And then there's the way you make me feel every time I see you walk into a room. Like the world is full of intriguing possibility. You make me feel like you and I are equally matched, in bed and out, sparring or comforting each other. Samantha Saffron Lilly of the three first names, I will never grow bored of you. I will never want to leave you. I'm sure of this." He kissed me. On the nose.

"I love you too. So much it hurts." I leaned into

him, my head against his chest, my cheek against the scratchy wool of his coat. "I didn't know it could feel like this. Now I know what my parents—" I broke off. Pulled away. Sat on the stoop, ignoring the cold against my butt.

Dylan sat too. "I'm not going to die, you know."

"You will, though. Someday you will." The words struggled to get past the tightness in my throat.

"And if I do, you'll survive. Because you're not your mother. You're stronger than her."

I blinked back a rush of heat behind my eyes, more tears on their way. "What if I'm not?"

"You are. Trust me. Anyone who built that sturdy a defense system? Is an amazingly strong woman."

The way he looked at me, so tender, so knowing— I did the only thing I could.

I kissed him, tasting the salt from my tears and the chill on both our lips along with a promise of passion, tonight and every night. Without hesitating for a single moment, he kissed me back, wrapping his arms around me. I squeezed him tight. So close. My heart on a string. My heart pounding against his. My heart wide open.

Above us, I heard a catcall. "It's about time, you two! But come up! Kiss on the couch. It's warmer."

I broke away from Dylan long enough to wave up at my roommate.

Dylan murmured against my hair, "She's right, you know."

"My bedroom is a mess. The apartment is grad-student casual. I can't—"

"Do you think I care?"

I smiled. "I guess not."

And I let him inside.

Epilogue

"Is that the last of them?" I closed the front door as Dylan's work buddy and his date clattered down the hall toward the elevator, and surveyed the messy aftermath. It had been a great party, but I was ready for something different. I walked up behind Dylan, who was busy cleaning up paper plates and plastic cups, and slipped my hands into his jeans. He startled, as if he'd forgotten he now lived with someone else—well, if *lived with* meant *had just started* and *now* meant right this minute. Then he relaxed and sighed against me. "I thought they'd never leave."

"Whose idea was this party, anyway?"

He turned and gave me a look brimming with amusement and meaning. "As I recall, *I* thought we should celebrate moving back in by throwing a raucous party of two. Naked. Right here." He kissed me and slid his hands up under my silky party shirt.

I hummed my pleasure against his chest. "Why didn't you veto me, then?"

"Because you've done a brilliant job with the apartment. I wanted to show it off. Fernando told me tonight that he's going to give you more challenging work now that he sees what you can do when you're let off leash." He grinned. "His words, not mine."

"Worth the long wait?" Dylan had to move out while the work was underway. He'd sublet a loft in Williamsburg. He claimed it gave him a chance to get familiarized with a new population of potential Juniper customers, and the fact that it was walking distance from my apartment was merely coincidental. He avoided my gaze as he said it, though, and his mouth twitched in a secret smile. I nailed him the next week by making him join our formerly all-female poker game. Jeanine won all his chips off him, Georgette psychoanalyzed him within an inch of his life, and Alanna teased him mercilessly while Annie peppered him with questions.

He passed all of it with flying colors. Which was when I told him yes, I would move in with him when this place was complete. He grinned and said how did I know he'd ask?

He pulled away from me now, folded his arms, and perused the space. "Hmm. Honestly? I think you left something out."

"*Now* you tell me?" I looked around, but I didn't have to. I knew every inch. The space was perfect. The new arch, the exposed wood of the crown molding, the tastefully remodeled kitchen that opened up to the dining room. I'd designed it all for Dylan. Everything I felt for him was in this living space.

So what was he talking about?

"It's okay. I know how to fix it."

I eyed him suspiciously. He looked serious, but the edge of his mouth twitched, a giveaway. Something was up.

He went down the hall to the linen closet and pulled something off the shelf, wrapped in brown paper. Curiouser and curiouser.

When he came back, he presented the package to me. It clattered heavily, like metal and wood and glass. "Think of it as a housewarming present." Dylan's gaze was warm, so warm.

I sat on the rug, ignoring the party debris around me, and tore open the package. Inside were three pictures. The one of me as Pirate Girl, one of my parents laughing together, and one of my grandparents squinting into the sun. They were all framed in old-fashioned cherrywood frames that suited them perfectly, but more—they'd all been restored. No creases, no stains. The ragged white line across my young pirate's chest was gone. Healed perfectly.

I looked up at him, my gaze blurry with tears. "You did this."

"Technically, our graphic design guy did it for me." But he was beaming. "I thought this place should have something of yours. It's yours now too, after all."

"And you vetoed my coffee table."

He winced, but it was for show. My old motley

coffee table was a long-running joke between us. I'd told him at one point that I thought we should model the design of all the furniture in his—now our—apartment after it. He'd fired me on the spot but rehired me minutes later when I'd offered to model the furniture in the nude.

I stood, holding the pictures like they might shatter if I wasn't careful. "Where should they go?" I looked around, but the answer was obvious. "The mantel."

I carefully set the three of them on the brand-new mantel, one by one, then stepped back. It was overwhelming to see them. Here. In my home. Our home. And yet…they were from the past, and this was my present.

"There's one more." Dylan stepped forward and placed a final framed shot on the ledge.

It was of the two of us, standing in Brooklyn Bridge Park last summer, the lower Manhattan skyline behind us, our arms wrapped around each other. In it, we were looking at each other, grinning like buffoons. We didn't look needy; we didn't look lost. We looked like we belonged.

Jeanine had taken the shot, and afterward we'd all gone on a boat ride to picnic and ride bikes around Governor's Island. A perfect late summer day.

Now, tonight, Dylan came up behind me and

wrapped his arms around me. "What do you think?"

I turned to him. "I think it's perfect." And it was.

And then I kissed him. Because I wanted to. Because I could. Because he was mine.

Author Note

Thank you for reading *Call Me Saffron*. I hope you enjoyed Samantha and Dylan's story.

You may be curious how this story came about. In particular, why a call girl?

Some years ago, I found an anonymous blog written by a graduate student moonlighting as a call girl to make money. She wrote a lot about her clients, mostly about her interactions with them and why they sought her out. It was clear that many of them saw her as a friend and confidante, filling an emotional need, not merely a sexual one.

Then last year, I read a piece in an online magazine by a woman who had been a sex worker and was now studying to become a nurse. When she told her friends, they said it made perfect sense. She'd always been drawn to the helping professions. Sex worker or nurse—in unexpected ways, the two are not so far apart.

I'm fascinated by the idea that sex can foster intimacy whether you intend it to or not. Because I write romance, not erotica or gritty literary tomes, I'm specifically drawn to that emotional, psychological puzzle. My heroines are not jaded, experienced sex workers (except for Jeanine). They're exploring their own sexuality, the intimate connection to another human being, and everything this brings up.

Want to find out when I have a new release? Sign up for my newsletter at http://taliasurova.com. I'll post news there first.

And please consider leaving a review on Amazon and/or Goodreads. They help other readers find books, and help authors find their footing. I appreciate all reviews.

Keep reading for descriptions of my other romances, followed by a description of *Pixel Perfect*, the first of a fun new mystery series, due out Winter 2015/2016.

Draw Me In

Struggling artist Raven Porter thought she'd learned to be tough the hard way. Now, though, she's arrived in New York City from rural Maine, and it's a whole new world.

With nowhere else to go, she crashes for the night in an empty warehouse. She wakes to the haunting sound of a lonely jazz saxophone. She's not alone.

Finn McKenna, proprietor of Finn's Fermentation Factory, needs to escape from his messy, complicated life, if only for tonight. So he flees to his warehouse and loses himself in his music. Until he realizes he's not alone.

Raven and Finn fit together. Two creative souls, their passions hidden behind sturdy defenses. If they can only let each other in...

Hold Me Tight

Alanna thought she'd never see Miles again. He was her first lover. The boy who broke her heart. But now he's the creative director at a high-profile ad agency and she's an impoverished artist. She needs the job he offers her.

Miles thinks he's gotten over Alanna. Brash, reckless, vivid Alanna. It's been eleven years, after all. When he hires her, he swears to himself that he'll keep away. For his own sake, and for the job: the office has a strict no-fraternizing policy.

Once they start working together, they're drawn to each other, tormented by what they can't have.

And then one sultry summer evening, a citywide blackout gives them an unexpected opportunity.

Tonight, in the dark, they can both pretend she's someone else. Tonight they can be together. A second chance at love, but a risky one.

Hold Me Tight won the RWA® Golden Heart for Contemporary Romance.

What's Yours is Mine

Darcy Jennings just bought a one bedroom condo, a gorgeous California cliffside property. It's the first time in her life she's had a permanent home, and it means everything to her. It's especially sweet after what happened four years ago. That's behind her now, and the rat who nearly ruined her career, one Will Dougherty, is history.

Will Dougherty just bought a one bedroom condo. He helped build the property with his green, clean designs, and this unit was mean to be his. It's up the road from his newly divorced sister, and it means everything to him. He's come a long way since the day his underhanded coworker, one Darcy Jennings, got him fired. Thankfully, he'll never have to see her again.

They couldn't be more wrong, as Darcy discovers when she stumbles into her condo after a long business trip, crawls into bed, and discovers a man there. Will Dougherty. And he says it's not her bed, it's his.

Now Will and Darcy have to live together twenty-four hours a day until one of them admits defeat. If only they could keep their hands off each other...

What's Yours is Mine was a RWA® Golden Heart
Finalist for Contemporary Romance.

Pixel Perfect

Book One of the Miranda Skye Mystery series

Budding photographer Miranda Skye thinks it's going to be an easy gig: return to her eccentric Catskills town, shoot a fancy faculty party at the local college as a favor to her dad, then sit down to a raucous family dinner.

And it *is* easy. Until she stumbles on the body. The one she just happens to capture in her camera's sights. The one that's going to wreak havoc on her father's career if the culprit isn't found, pronto.

The local cops think sexy bad boy Donovan James, aka Miranda's high school nemesis, did the deed. Which should delight her. Except that she has a niggling feeling they're arresting the wrong man.

And for some strange reason, she feels the need to exonerate him.

(And no, that kiss has nothing to do with it.)

(Nothing at all.)

Sign up for my newsletter at www.taliasurova.com to be alerted when *Pixel Perfect* is released.

Acknowledgements

This book, with its racy premise, was something of a departure for me, and I want to thank Diane Patterson in particular for encouraging me to give it a go.

Thanks to Daniel Valverde, my first and always reader. To my talented writer friends Sonali Dev, Amy Patrick, Alaya Johnson, and AJ Larrieu for the insightful notes and the shot of confidence. And to my sharp-eyed editor, Linda Ingmanson.

I'm grateful to have such intelligent people watching my back.

About the Author

Talia Surova began her writing career as a screenwriter but switched to prose after she started writing an online journal for fun. This led to writing fiction, which led to writing romance.

She is a two-time finalist for the prestigious Romance Writers of America® Golden Heart award, and won the Golden Heart in 2012 for *Hold Me Tight*, then titled *No Peeking*.

After a long detour to Southern California, she now lives in New York City, her childhood hometown, with her husband and son.